THE MYSTERY OF THE MOONSTONE

A Metaphysical Primer

Carolyn Stearns

Edited by the CreateSpace Staff
And Christopher May

Printed in the United States of America

ISBN: 1450583229
ISBN 13: 9781450583220
Library of Congress Control Number: 2012906925
CreateSpace Independent Publishing Platform
North Charleston, South Carolina

For Maddie,

who sees the grass grow

ACKNOWLEDGMENT

I once had a friend whose name was Adam, a young lad who chose me to be his godmother. When he approached 10 and I was 50, his mother asked what he wanted for his 10th birthday. He said, "A massage by Carolyn," something his mother enjoyed once a month. Adam was given his birthday wish. He repeated his wish year after year until he and his mother moved away when he was 15.

During our sessions together, we drew pictures, talked, shared dreams, and bounced up and down on two big yellow balls while his mother, a psychotherapist, sat in the corner of the room and watched.

In short order, Adam was sharing his conversations with his spiritual playmates with me. His secret life was rich and wonderful except for one thing: he thought he was weird. None of his friends had spiritual experiences quite like his.

It was then I decided to write this book. I wanted Adam to see he wasn't weird or crazy, but rather, he was blessed, and what was happening to him was perfectly normal.

Adam is no longer in my life. He is probably married now, with children of his own. I wonder if he knows how much he taught me, how much I learned during those most unusual massage sessions. I'll make sure he gets a copy of the book.

C. S.
September 2014

CHAPTER ONE

When I was little, my father told me our summer cottage beside a wonderful lake in the Canadian woods was haunted. He told me stories about the ghost of a poor young maiden who wandered about at night looking for her long lost love.

Because of stories like that one, I tried to avoid thoughts of ghosts ever since I was five years old. Thinking of them when I was at the lake scared me so badly that for several years I refused to go to the outhouse alone after dark. I thought someone would grab me or a bobcat would jump out of the trees and eat me.

By the time I was 13, I'm happy to report I went to the outhouse by myself after dark, and I rarely thought about those ghost stories. Then, however, everything changed.

Here is what happened.

That summer when I was 13, while my mother and father and I were at the lake on our vacation, my parents decided to return briefly to Toronto, our home city, to visit my Granny Rose, who was very sick. I am Granny Rose's namesake. So people don't mix us up, everyone calls me Rosie, except when they're angry at me. Then they call me Rosalie Ann. Ann is my middle name.

My parents surprised me by letting me stay in the cottage by myself while they were gone. They agreed I would be better off at the lake than I would be in the city, where they'd be busy looking after Granny Rose and I'd be alone, rattling around in our townhouse, wondering what to do.

"Still, what if there is a storm?" my mother asked. "You hate storms."

"Not to worry," I answered bravely.

"We'll only be gone for a few days," said Mom, looking at Dad with a worried expression. "At most a week."

"Go," I insisted. I loved the idea of having the cottage to myself. "If there's a storm, I'll cross my fingers and toes, bury my head under a pillow, and be fine."

"We won't be gone long," said my father, whose brow was as wrinkled as my mom's. "As soon as Granny Rose feels better, Rosie, we'll be back. You be careful now -- be the good camper we know you are."

'Yes! Yes! Of course I will!"

"And remember, don't swim out to Gull Rock by yourself. It's too far."

"I won't."

I knew they wanted to warn me about many other possible dangers, but they didn't. I was glad they restrained themselves.

My mother and father would never have let me stay alone if Doc hadn't been close. He's a hermit who lives in a log cabin in the next cove. Everyone calls him the Hermit of the Lake because he lives alone and is at the lake most of the year.

"I know the lake and woods at least as well as you do," I told my parents. "You and Doc have taught me well. Anyway, I'm certain Mrs. McCrae will be dropping by to check up on me. What more can I say? I'll be fine."

But on the night after they left, I stopped feeling so confident. Strange things happened I couldn't explain, things that never happened when my parents were there. The hand water pump at the sink started pumping by itself while I was in bed. I could hear it. I also heard the icebox door open and close.

The next morning I found a pad and pencil carefully placed on the dining table; I knew I hadn't put them there.

These happenings made me think a lot about the ghost maiden in my father's stories, more than was probably helpful since I was in the cottage alone.

Actually, I was not totally by myself. I had our Siberian husky, Cassie, and our cats, Lizzie and Twyla, with me. But I couldn't talk with them about ghosts.

On the evening of my second day alone, I paddled down the lake to see Doc.

"Doc!"

I call him Doc because that is what my mother and father call him. My father said he used to be a doctor, but his patients decided he didn't have a good enough bedside manner, so he quit.

"Doc! Where are you?"

I love Doc. He talks to all of the plants in his garden, and he knows many, many bird calls. People on the lake think he's a little crazy, although they never say so when they need his medical advice.

Doc manages to spend his winters in jail on minor charges to avoid the harsh winter weather, but he comes back to the lake in the spring in plenty of time to start his garden and greet his friends the birds. I've known him ever since I was a little girl. He is my father's oldest friend.

"Doc!"

Finally I spotted him between two red cedars. Doc is a short man and looks like a troll. He never wears shoes, which makes it seem as though he's just gotten out of bed. He has a prickly gray beard, and he always wears overalls, the kind train engineers wear, the kind I wear. He beckoned me to his dock.

"Oh, Doc, I'm glad you're here. There have been some mysterious goings on in my cottage since my mother and father left."

Doc tied my canoe to the dock with a special lake knot. He never says a word that isn't absolutely one hundred percent necessary. I think he's the wisest person I know -- well, not as wise as my dad.

I told him about the water pump and the icebox door and the pad and pencil, hoping he'd say something profound, but he didn't. He just smiled in his most mysterious way.

"Do you suppose the cottage is haunted?" I asked.

I watched as Doc fed a chipmunk a peanut.

"Are you paying attention?" I asked impatiently.

Finally, he spoke.

"It sounds to me as if you had company, Rosie. You must be ready for a teacher."

"Really?" I asked.

"Yep. A guide. If he or she comes again, don't be afraid. Fear keeps us in the dark."

"Is this guide or teacher visible, or is it like a ghost?" I asked.

The hermit shrugged. "That depends on you," he said.

I followed Doc down to my favorite log, where we sat and watched the sun go down behind some dark clouds that were beginning to gather. I hoped he would say more, but he didn't.

"Thanks a heap, Doc," I said a little sarcastically as the sun disappeared. I was sure disappointment was written all over my face. I wanted him to tell me what to do. I wondered what my father would say if he were here. I stomped down to the dock and eased myself back into my canoe.

"Everything is as it needs to be," said Doc philosophically as he untied my canoe. "Remember, fear keeps us in the dark."

Doc pushed me off and I headed home.

*

I love our cottage. I love it because we have no running water, no electricity, no telephone, no roads, none of those things I take for granted in the city. One can only get to our cottage by water.

I couldn't have telephoned Doc or Mrs. McCrae even if there had been an emergency.

It was a short paddle back to my cottage, but long enough for me to pick up the continuing signs that a storm was brewing. From the looks of the leaves turned inside out on the trees (Doc would say the trees were showing their petticoats) and the absence of birds, my guess was it was going to be a big one. The sky was eerily dark.

My mother is right, I hate storms. When I got home, I walked the boundaries of the peninsula to check that everything was secure. I made certain the family outboard motorboat was tied tightly to our dock, and then hauled the canoe into the woods and tied it to a tree. I put Lizzie, Twyla and Cassie inside the cottage. At that moment I wished I had human company. I knew I'd never tell my mother and father I felt that way or they'd never allow me to stay alone again.

Flashes of lightning began to split the dark sky, and distant peals of thunder followed. The wind rose, pushing the storm along. I retreated into the cottage and lit a kerosene lamp. The waves splashed onto the rocks outside.

I wished I were one of those people who like storms. Some people do. My father does. When I was three, he woke me up so I could see an honest-to-goodness hurricane blowing down the center of our street in the city.

"Hobbit Head," (his nickname for me because my hair is so dark and curly), "look at the way the rain comes pounding down toward us. You'll probably never see a hurricane this close again." A big tree crashed against the garage in our back yard. My mother screamed and pleaded with us to come inside.

"You never have to be afraid of a storm, Hobbit Head."

Now I was in the cottage alone, I was terrified. I had been afraid of storms even before I heard about the ghost maiden.

Stop thinking about her, I scolded myself.

7

What does she look like anyway? Does she glow in the dark? Does she look like Casper in the comic strips?

"Stop it!" I said out loud.

I found a second kerosene lamp and lit it. The extra light helped me feel safe. The old, worn cottage furniture looked friendly in the soft glow of the lamps.

Tree branches scraped their wooden fingers over the roof of the cottage. No night animals prowled that night. It was too dark, too windy.

The thunder got louder. The storm came closer. Each clap of thunder felt stronger than the last. I worried the ghost maiden would walk past one of the windows at any moment.

"Stop it!" I said out loud. "Stop thinking about ghosts. Find something fun to do, and then the storm will hurry by." My mother would have said that if she had been there.

I decided to start hooking a new tapestry.

My rug-latching equipment was in an old sea chest Granny Rose gave me. I wondered how she was. I opened the chest and took out my last empty canvas backing and several bundles of two inch pieces of yarn. Each piece was left over from other projects I had started but never finished. I had many different colors -- red, orange, blue, lots of green, an ugly yellow, black, and a soft shade of brown, like tanned leather.

I carried everything to the table by the south windows and sat down to make piles of each of the different colors. I examined my canvas backing for the tapestry. It was blank. So was my mind. I decided to let this tapestry design itself.

Scrape went the branches on the roof.

Bang went the family tin boat against the dock.

Cassie scurried under the couch.

Lizzie and Twyla hovered close to the lamps.

I looked out the window. It was so dark I couldn't see the light from the lighthouse on the opposite side of the lake. It was as if a black blanket had dropped suddenly over the house.

Cassie sighed deeply. I could tell it was a sigh of resignation. She doesn't like storms any more than I do. They are as scary as balloons, she would have said if she could talk. She hates balloons.

The lightning was bright as it zigged and zagged across the sky. The thunder began to get into my bones. I knew it was already raining on the opposite shore. In the daytime, I love to watch the rain move across the lake like a great wall.

I looked at my watch. 8 PM. Now it was pitch black outside, when normally the sun's rays would still be coloring the western sky.

The first drops of rain splattered on the roof in big splashy drops. The wind pushed a light spray of rain into the house. Some of my little strands of tapestry yarn were whipped into the air and dropped like feathers onto the floor. I got up and closed the cottage windows.

The lightning was pretty in its way -- it was the thunder that frightened me. I used to think God was taking the night off to go bowling when it thundered. At other times I thought God was angry with me and when He was done bowling He would come to punish me for lying, or being a bad daughter. I decided I liked it better having the windows closed. It was quieter.

I picked up a piece of red yarn and hooked it to the empty canvas at random, close to the middle. Red is my favorite color. It has been ever since I was given my first box of crayons.

Suddenly, I remembered that in a storm the ghost maiden sang. She got bolder! I trembled, and added more yarn to the canvas with clammy fingers.

The click-click sound of my hooker was barely audible. The wind outside sounded almost human.

All I could see of Cassie was her tail. She thought she was safe under the couch. Should I tell her that her tail was sticking out? Lizzie and Twyla were bathing each other, finding comfort, as I did, in the light and warmth of the lamps.

Click-click.

It didn't matter what color I picked that night.

Click-click.

The color red made me feel alert.

Click-click. Click-click.

Now the center of the storm was over the cottage. The roof chattered as it received the full impact of the wind and rain. The lightning and thunder came so closely together it was hard to separate the two.

I prayed no trees would fall on the cottage. I started singing to drown out the sound of the banging clouds. I kept hooking.

Click-click. Click-click.

I picked another color, blue. Blue was more soothing than red.

I am doing pretty well, I thought to myself. I was not nearly as afraid as I usually was. In the past, thunder sent me dashing under the bed covers, night or day, so God wouldn't find me, bad me.

Click-click.

I couldn't do that on this night. This night I was a grown-up. I was glad the animals were close to keep me company.

Click-click.

The thunder made me feel small, freckly, and powerless. I put on a large, plaid-flannel shirt for comfort. It was a shirt my father gave me for my birthday.

Knock. Knock.

Clearly, that wasn't thunder. I felt a chill enter my spine.

Knock. Knock. Knock.

I stopped hooking. I didn't move. The chill invaded my chest.

Knock. Knock. Knock.

No one could be out on a night like this, I thought. An image of the ghost maiden flitted through my mind. I made the picture go away.

I looked at the door. There was no lock. Doc couldn't help me. No one could help me now.

Maybe it was a branch banging against the roof.

Knock. Knock. Knock. Knock.

That was no branch. It was definitely a knock.

Knock. Knock. Knock. Knock.

"Who's there?" I heard myself ask. My voice sounded hollow, as if the room were an echo chamber. "Tell me who's there." I felt like the third little pig.

Knock. Knock. Knock. Knock. Knock. Knock.

I got up from my chair and walked toward the door on the north side of the house. I looked at Cassie under the couch. She was sleeping soundly. Some protector she was.

I placed my hand on the door knob. But before I could turn it, I quickly pulled my hand back. The door knob was warm. Whatever or whoever was on the other side of the door was generating a lot of heat. I felt a strange energy, as if the door itself were pulsating slightly. The door actually felt alive.

"Who's there?" I repeated a little more boldly this time. My heart was pounding so vigorously that my chest felt as if it were going to crack open. Lightning flickered and lit the sky, with thunder responding with bangs like fire crackers. The cats watched intently, their tails fluffed out like fat sausages.

Finally, I decided the suspense of not knowing who was outside the door was worse than knowing. I took a deep breath and turned the knob, stepping backward as the door swung into the room.

The light from the kerosene lamps shone out into the night. I had a caller. It was not the ghost maiden. I instantly felt more confident.

My visitor was a man. He was soaking wet, glistening with the rain. He smiled as if we were old friends. He projected heat, like the lamps. He did not look like any teacher I knew. But who in the world was he? I shivered with a pang of fear.

My father would have asked him in right away. My father always said if someone came to the door when we were in the woods, it would be a camper in need of help. But I was alone. My mother would have told me not to let him in, to lock and bolt the door. But I had no lock. I had no bolt. Why should I have? What was there to lock out, a porcupine?

I kept staring.

My visitor kept smiling. He didn't look injured or dangerous.

Doc had said not to be afraid.

The man wore a red-and-black-checked wool jacket, faded jeans and great heavy lumberjack's boots. His face was full of shadows from the light of the flickering lamps. His cheekbones seemed hand-carved. He looked a little like an Indian, with black, penetrating eyes. But his hair wasn't like an Indian's at all. It was long and white, flowing down around his shoulders. He was probably quite old, yet his face was unlined.

I decided I had to do something, so I tentatively extended my hand. Shaking hands seemed like something my mother might have done. I looked into his face. I liked his eyes.

As soon as we touched, I felt confused, as if I were suddenly turning upside down. His hand didn't feel like a hand at all, even though it looked like one. His hand was hot, and it felt as if he were wearing a glove.

I studied the hand hard. It was resilient, like soft, spongy, foam rubber. A feeling of energy moved up my arm and into the rest of my body.

My visitor remained calm, as if he were neither worried nor embarrassed about standing at my door in the middle of a storm in the dark of night. His eyes said I should trust him.

Neither of us moved. He stayed on the outside, and I stayed in. But it felt the other way around, as if I were the one standing on the outside. I decided to invite the stranger in.

A big raindrop splashed from the roof onto my visitor's nose. He continued to smile, not saying a word. The wind blew his hair flat against his cheek.

"Come inside," I finally said. "I'll build you a fire."

He stepped in and I closed the door behind him.

"Who are you?" I asked. "I don't know you."

We stood about three feet apart. I couldn't tell what he wanted or needed because he didn't speak. He made Doc seem like a regular chatterbox. I looked down at his wet boots. What I saw surprised me. His boots weren't made of leather. They looked as if they were made of cloth, as if they were part of his pants.

I looked higher, and with closer inspection I saw his jacket was part of his shirt. These weren't real clothes, at least not like any I had ever seen. True, on the outside he was wearing a lumberjack's outfit, but it was a cover. He was wearing a one-piece suit, like the unitard I wear to dance class. All his clothing was of a piece: his jacket, his jeans, his boots, his bright green turtleneck shirt. Everything. Even his shoelaces!

I looked back at his face, hoping he would explain. All he did was smile and nod.

I started to build a fire, grateful for something to do. I wished the storm would let up so the house would stop shuddering. My visitor didn't seem bothered by anything, not even his wet clothes.

"This is some storm," I said self-consciously as I tucked my hair behind my ears. He sneezed and I practically jumped out of my skin.

I crumpled up some old newspapers for kindling.

My visitor remained standing in the center of the room while I laid the fire. I wished he would stop staring and start talking.

"Who are you?" I asked again. I was losing patience.

I tried to keep my annoyance out of my voice. The stranger's silence was making me anxious. But his eyes were searching and kind. They looked gently inquisitive, the way Cassie's do when she is watching a fish flop on the bottom of the tin boat.

When I saw the fire was going to burn without smoking up the cottage, I guided my silent visitor to one of the chairs close to the fire.

I put my hand on the man's arm. It too was warm, and once again those perplexing feelings moved through me. I didn't know why, but initially I didn't pull my hand away; I kept it right where it was.

I could see the stranger's face more clearly now. I looked closely to see if he might talk with his eyes.

Yikes!

His eyes weren't real either! They must be painted on, I thought, like his clothes, his nose, his mouth, his teeth. His whole face was a mask. His hair, even his ears, were part of the covering. The whites of his eyes were painted to look slightly bloodshot, and there was a dimple painted on the center of his chin. He looked as if he were wearing a big painted tarpaulin.

I jerked my hand away from his arm. I was too stunned to ask him to sit, even though he was standing in front of one of the wingback chairs.

Maybe I should ask this creature to leave, I thought. Or, maybe I should pretend my mother and father are in their bedroom. I wished Cassie were a better guard dog.

Finally, my visitor spoke in short, choppy sentences, all said with the same intonation. "I hope my attire is appropriate. Would you like me better if I became someone else?"

Who said that, I wondered? I saw his mouth move, but the words didn't come from between his lips. Yet I knew what I heard were his words. Something inside me told me that.

I answered the only way I knew how, by speaking out loud the way I talk with my friends.

"No, you look fine. Just tell me who you are."

I struggled not to shriek. Even his smile was painted on. If only he'd explain. Who was he? Why was he here? What did he want?

"Here, put this around you."

I handed him a wool blanket that matched the wingback chairs. "I'll make us some tea. Maybe then you'll feel like telling me who you are."

My visitor took the blanket. He looked befuddled, as if he didn't know what to do with it. The thunder was making it increasingly difficult for us to talk.

I went to the stove and lit the burner under the kettle to boil water. I pulled out two mugs, a tea pot, and a tray. My visitor still hadn't moved. He continued standing awkwardly with the blanket in one of his hands. I returned to the fire.

As I put on another log, Cassie decided to join us at last. I heard her rabies and identification tags jangling as she struggled to come out from under the couch. Cassie's curiosity about the stranger was overcoming her fear of thunder.

17

Cassie stretched. She looked at the stranger, and walked fearlessly toward him. She wagged her white-tipped, curled husky tail and pressed her ears flat against her head. She wiggled her whole body in greeting, with the same sort of coquettishness she saves for my friends; she says hello this way when she wants to play.

Cassie liked the stranger. She decided this even without first inspecting him with her nose.

My guest sat down in the chair, and Cassie turned around and sat on the man's foot while lifting her nose high in the air, toward the man's knee. This is a very trusting gesture for any dog, particularly a husky.

Yeow!

The lightning was close. Its blue-white light surrounded the cottage, and the claps of thunder were unrelenting in their intensity. Cassie nudged and pushed to get closer to the stranger, to feel safer. At the next crack of thunder, I noticed smoke in the room. I looked up anxiously to see if the roof was on fire. When I saw it wasn't, I realized the smoke was coming out of the fireplace. The only way to get rid of the smoke was to open the windows. Bother, then the rain would come in.

The smoke got worse. Suddenly there was a quick, bright flash of light with an instant crack of thunder, and a tree crashed in the woods. I jumped, the cats leapt off the table, and Cassie cowered against the leg of my guest. Bad, bad me forgot, momentarily, the sound of thunder meant I was safe. All I saw was smoke. Instantly I got up to open the windows.

What had happened? The windows were already open.

I stopped in my tracks. I looked back at the stranger; could he have done this? But he was sitting in the chair by the fire with the blanket still in his hand. Cassie hadn't moved either. She was still sitting on his foot, looking eager for a touch from the man's hand.

"Thank you," I said, figuring he must have opened the windows somehow or other. But how did he leave his chair without my seeing him do so, without Cassie moving?

I noticed a quiet, yellow light around the edges of the stranger's body. The warmth I felt in his hand and on his arm was probably moving throughout his body for him to glow this way. I put my hand down on my yarn and canvas.

"Do not worry," the stranger said. "Nothing is getting wet. Please notice the fire has stopped smoking."

Again the stranger seemed to talk without speaking.

I felt the table and my chair next to the windows. Both were dry. He was right. Not a drop of water was coming in. My canvas and yarn were completely dry.

"I will close the windows if you like," I sensed him say.

I looked at him untrustingly, but nodded yes, anyway.

I saw another flash of lightning and heard another snap-crack of thunder. Again I jumped, even though I tried not to. For a moment I wondered if the lightning had hit me, but that was only a fleeting thought. When

I looked back at the windows, they were tightly closed.

"Wow!" I exclaimed, smiling in spite of my questions.

I looked at the stranger differently, realizing he not only heard me, but he knew what I was thinking! Now he was scratching Cassie's white fur beneath her chin. I wished I knew how to talk to him. Maybe I should try writing.

Immediately, as if I had spoken these thoughts, the stranger sat with a pencil and a pad, the very ones I discovered on my table yesterday morning. Still he had not left his chair.

I was right! He could read my mind.

No thank you, I thought, and I watched the pad and pencil magically disappear.

The kettle whistled shrilly.

"The water's hot!"

I hurried to the stove to turn off the flame. I postponed my questions until the water was poured over the teabags. I removed the lid of the screeching kettle.

Slowly I started to pour the hot water into the teapot and as I did, a medium-sized brown spider scurried out of the teapot's nozzle.

"Bad spider!" I cried.

Without thinking, I knocked the spider on to the floor, and killed it instantly with my foot. For my whole life I had hated spiders. Spiders made me as jumpy as thunder, as afraid as ghost maidens.

This was not the time to think about spiders or ghosts. I had a guest to think about. I wondered: could he drink the tea with his painted mouth? Would he need a straw?

When the pot was full, I put it on the tray with the two mugs and turned back toward my guest, suspecting he had heard my thoughts about straws and probably spiders, too.

The visitor was gone.

"Hey!" I shrieked. "Where are you?"

The wool blanket was in a heap on the floor in front of the blazing fire. Cassie was on the blanket, curled up in her serious sleep position with her tail draped over her nose, as if she'd been there all night.

The back door banged. My eyes followed the sound and I saw the door swinging forward and back. The rain was pouring in hard.

I closed the door with my free hand and went back to the fire and put my tea tray down on the floor. I sat in the chair my visitor had been sitting in. It was still warm.

Cassie wagged her tail slightly. She was not at all unnerved. The storm was beginning to pass. I was certain she knew that.

I poured myself some tea and stared into the fire. I needed answers. Who was my visitor, anyway? Why had he left so suddenly, without saying good-bye? And why hadn't I seen him go?

I sat that way for a long time until my body felt stiff and the tea in my mug was cold. The thunder and lightning drifted way off and the wind was finally still.

I looked at my watch for the second time. 11:30 PM.

I felt chilled. Instead of stirring up the fire, I decided to go to bed. Cassie sensed my decision and headed into the bedroom. I heard her push her body into the small space between the bed boards and the floor as I brushed my teeth.

Who was the stranger, and where did he go? Where did he come from? And what was his name? By then I was beginning to feel more and more annoyed, which led me to anger. What did he mean by coming to my door in the midst of a storm? Why didn't he tell me who he was? That was very rude of him. Clearly he couldn't be the guide or teacher Doc told me about.

Before I blew out the lamps, I absentmindedly picked up the blanket that was still in a heap on the floor by the chair. A small object fell from inside its folds and landed between my feet on the braided rug in front of the fireplace.

I looked down at a white stone, about half the size of my thumbnail. I picked it up carefully. It captured the light and energy of the smoldering coals. I recognized it: it was a moonstone.

The stone was warm, just as the door knob had been, just as my guest's hand and arm had been. The stone, too, felt alive. I dropped it immediately.

Now that's silly, I thought. It's just a stone. I picked it up again and walked over to the kerosene lamp so I could see it better.

As I held the stone under the light, I could almost see through it. It was murky, milky, semi-transparent. It looked very old and worn, as if it had tumbled about on the bottom of the lake or a river for centuries. Where did it come from? Why was it here? All I had were questions, just as I had when my visitor was here.

"This is definitely a moonstone," I announced to the cats. "It's not your ordinary stone. I'm sure of it!"

I looked more closely. This time I saw an eye etched in the narrow end of the stone. The moonstone was looking at me, just as my visitor had done. My evening was moving from strange to bizarre.

Could this be a present from my visitor, I thought to myself, a thank you for taking him in out of the rain? A part of me wished the stranger had stayed so I could ask him. But then I had a second thought: that was too weird. I didn't want the stranger back again.

I blew out the lamps and went into the bedroom. I kept the moonstone in my hand. I was beginning to like the feel of it, its warmth and its pulse. I held it respectfully as I slipped between the cool sheets.

I looked out the window. The rain had stopped. I could see the light from the lighthouse across the lake. The stone seemed to be telling me I was safe and protected.

I reached over and opened the window by my bed, and let the night air move gently over my face. The lake was silent as if it were winter.

The stranger has gone, I thought. A good thing. If only I knew what to call him. Did he know my name was Rosie? No matter. I'll never open the door to a stranger again. It's too risky. I'm lucky no harm came to me. I'll ask Doc if he'll kindly put a lock on my door.

I love the feeling of safety when I'm in my bed. I rolled over onto my left side and fell asleep.

CHAPTER TWO

When I woke up the next morning, Cassie was asleep on the bed at my feet, Lizzie was pressing close to my cheek, and Twyla was nestled along the curve of my back, down near my waist. As we leaned against each other, I knew the night had turned cold. Otherwise, Cassie would have been under the bed and the cats would have been sitting on the window sill, watching the morning define itself. They get cuddly when they need warmth, aloof when they don't.

I opened my eyes a crack. I didn't need to open them very wide to see the day was a beautiful one. The air was so clean the blue sky looked as bright as the sun. The trees sparkled with rain drops, balancing on the leaves like tiny crystals as they dropped from the sky. The sun was a nine o'clock sun, and the wind was already blowing at a crisp rate. I could feel a touch of fall in the air.

As soon as I stirred under the blankets, Cassie jumped off the bed, Lizzie complained she needed to be fed, and Twyla pressed closer, urging me to stay where I was.

"Come on Twy, move! It's time to get up."

My voice sent Lizzie to the floor. Twyla stayed exactly where she was.

I sat up in bed with a start. All the memories of the night before came rushing back to me. I reviewed every minute of my time with the creepy stranger, feeling very fortunate he hadn't hurt me. I looked outside -- I could barely believe the world had been so black and threatening only a little while ago.

I flung myself down on my pillow and began to laugh. My oh my, will I never grow up? Dad would have gotten a big laugh if he had seen me shivering and shaking because of a little thunder and lightning. But no, that wasn't true. He wouldn't have laughed at all if I told him about opening the door to a stranger in the dark of night.

Suddenly, I remembered the moonstone. Where was it?

I hurriedly searched my bed. I wanted proof I really had had a caller. I felt all around, in between and under the covers, the sheets, even the bedspread.

Twyla jumped off the bed with an irritated meow. I felt around with my fingers and toes. I looked under the pillow. I looked in the folds of my flannel nighty. I couldn't find the moonstone anywhere.

I stood up in bed and shook my nighty loose from around me. I shook my body in case the moonstone had gotten stuck to my skin. I checked the pockets in my nightgown. I shook my head. I even shook a spare blanket heaped under the window sill at the foot of the bed. I looked everywhere.

The moonstone was nowhere to be found.

Maybe I made the whole thing up. Maybe I went to bed early . . .maybe it was a dream . . .maybe . . . .

I got out of bed and dressed quickly so the cold air wouldn't cool my skin. Since I was alone, I didn't bother to brush my hair or teeth. I put on a pair of sneakers -- no socks -- and gathered the animals. We all walked out into the morning air. The cats, looking sullen, scurried under the house to take care of business. They hated it when I made them go outside without feeding them first.

Cassie bounded ahead adventurously as I walked toward the back rock. That is my favorite wake-up place on a cold morning -- it is sheltered from the wind and I can count on the sun to warm me.

Cassie went faster than I, cutting through the underbrush. I took the path, weaving my way under an awning of evergreen trees. I could feel the water from the night's rain spilling onto my sleeves and rubbing off on my pant legs. Clearly, I hadn't dreamt the rain.

I picked up a walking stick and swung it before me like a sword, breaking the spider webs that might stick to or tickle my nose. I hated spider webs as much as I hated spiders. I never walked down a path in the woods without a stick.

When I arrived at the back rock, Cassie was already wading in the lake and drinking water, an important part of her morning ritual. The sun was so bright I wished I had remembered my old Brooklyn Dodgers baseball cap to shade my eyes. However, I didn't want to take the time to go back for it because I had a lot to think about, a lot to process. I made a visor with my hand.

The rock felt untroubled as I stepped onto it. It always feels that way. That's why it's my favorite rock. I think of this particular rock as royalty because it has a vein of milky white quartz about five inches wide running diagonally through its center. I usually stand or sit on its hump where the quartz is the thickest. That's where I think my innermost thoughts. That's my special place.

I like my quiet time in the morning. Sometimes I sit looking at the water. Sometimes I let the sun gently massage my shoulders. The rock, the sun, the water, and the air give me what I need, even if I don't know what that happens to be. I feel safe in the sunlight.

Would the stranger come back? If he did, what should I do then? Should I stay with Mrs. McCrae tonight? I couldn't stay with Doc.

I slowly gave myself to the rock. If I had gotten up earlier, I would have gone to the dock for my quiet time and watched the water lilies open. Doc taught me to do that. On warm mornings, I usually sit on the front rock, watching little waves form as the wind brushes against the lake's surface. Always I go where it is quiet, and always it is important that I not be disturbed.

"Don't bother me for the next hour," I would say to my parents.

"The peninsula is yours," my mother would answer. "Your father and I are going fishing."

I could tell by the way they looked at each other they were sure I would one day be a hermit, like Doc.

On this particular morning, I was glad I was alone, really alone. I didn't have to worry about someone inadvertently barging in on my quiet time. That was what I liked best about having the cottage to myself. First, I had to think about the stranger. Second, I had to think about the moonstone and its disappearance. What was last night all about?

Without knowing why, I found myself staring at the bottom of the lake. I could see sand, lake grass, rocks, and several boulders. The water is so clear and clean that I often drink from it the way Cassie does, only instead of lapping it up with my tongue, I inhale water as if I were kissing the lake.

My eyes were looking for something my brain wasn't certain existed. Every now and again, I saw something shiny in the water that sent up a bright ray of light. It looked as if the lake might have a precious jewel hidden among its smaller stones.

I squinted my eyes to see better. I saw it again. I thought of the moonstone. Don't be silly; I lost the moonstone in my bed -- if, indeed, there ever was a moonstone.

I quickly took off my sweatshirt, rolled up my pants and shirtsleeves, kicked off my sneakers and waded to the little spark of light. I stepped fast because I don't like the feeling of silt oozing between my toes.

The water was cold, in sharp contrast to the morning sun. When my feet got to the spot where my eyes told them to stop, I reached down with my hand and fumbled among the water plants, clam shells and larger rocks. It was deeper than I thought. The water splashed against my shoulder joint. My shirtsleeve got soaked.

I felt something smooth.

"I think I've got it!" I shouted to Cassie.

Cassie ignored me.

Whatever it was felt warm, even under the cold water. I stood up. In my hand was a familiar-looking milky white stone, glowing with energy and life. The lake water bumped cheerfully against my legs.

The stone looked and felt like the moonstone I found last night! Its warmth said it was. But how did it get out here? What was happening? What was going on?

I walked back to the shore and sat down on the rock in the center of the quartz line. Without putting the stone down, I slipped off my wet shirt and put on the sweatshirt warming in the sun. I unrolled my pant legs and pressed my feet onto the warm rock.

When I was comfortable, I inspected the stone again -- this time more carefully. I held it up toward the sun so I could see all of its markings.

It was my moonstone, milky and smooth! I was sure of it. The eye was there, still looking at me. I could never confuse this stone with another. Last night was real. It was not just a dream.

I remembered when Doc found a special stone like this one, he always put it on his third eye, the space on his forehead above his nose and between his eyebrows. He said stones held memories, pictures from long ago.

"Stones can lead you to an inner world," he told me once. Even a moonstone, I now wondered?

I decided to do what Doc did, hoping he was right, hoping the stone would tell me how it got from my bed into the lake.

I pressed the moonstone tightly against my skin, exactly as I remembered seeing Doc do it. I was surprised at the way its warmth immediately spread across my brow. The heat made me feel happy, so happy I forgot to be afraid. I kept the moonstone on my forehead and closed my eyes and lay back on the rock.

I don't know how long I stayed that way; I felt so comfortable. Who cared if I received pictures the way Doc does, or not? Who cared who the stranger was? I was enjoying feeling at peace with myself and the world. The rock beneath me fit the curve of my back perfectly.

Soon I could see movement in the back side of my closed eyes. The more I concentrated, the more I was sure something was starting to happen. I saw a lot of light and many different shades of green.

My body felt lighter, as if the rock were pushing up against my spine. The sound of the water lapping against the rock became more distant, and I stopped worrying about ants crawling over me and tickling my feet.

The picture got clearer. I saw a lot of things moving around in a circle -- were they stones? -- swirling and circling, creating patterns like the ones I used to make with finger paints.

After a harder look, I changed my mind. They were not stones. They looked more like turtles. I saw heads and legs. Yes, I was certain of it. They were turtles.

The longer I concentrated, the sharper the picture became. I could see little arms and legs as the turtles danced around in their shell-houses. They seemed to be following one another like a parade of elephants, going round and round, doing do-si-do movements like the moves I learned in gym class.

One turtle danced alone in the center of the circle until it abruptly stopped, spun around, and dropped low onto a high mound of bright green moss.

As if that were a signal, the other turtles stopped dancing and spun around in the same way, until they dropped onto the ground. The turtle in the center of the circle quickly pulled its head, arms, legs and tail inside its shell.

My eyes remained riveted on the center of the circle. Every now and then the center turtle stuck its head out of its shell to see if the other turtles were happily settled on the earth.

Suddenly, all was still. The turtle shells resembled a gathering of tepees. I wondered what the turtles did and thought inside their shells. Many of them kept peeking out to see what was going on.

I was sure an artist would have loved to paint what I saw -- I had never seen so many bright, vibrant colors. Even the earth tones popped out at me with surprising brilliance. The green color of the moss would be pretty in the tapestry I was making.

I guessed there was water close by, because two young frogs watched from behind a stone. They were hard to see because they were as bright a green as the moss and the grass. Their eyes showed some of the excitement I felt. They looked as if they were waiting for something or someone.

Beyond the turtles, I recognized many of the different herbs Doc grows in his garden -- King Comfrey, Sir Basil, Queen Sage, Lady Calendula. They all swayed rhythmically to sounds I could only imagine. Every now and again I got a whiff of lavender mixed with rosemary, the princesses of Doc's garden. I wondered if the turtles, the frogs, and the many flowers and herbs knew I could see them.

How strange to be so close and yet feel so far away. I wanted to let them know I was there and would like to join them.

All of a sudden, a majestic American bald eagle appeared out of the blue. The circled turtles popped their heads out of their shells to watch, though the center turtle did not. The eagle took great pleasure gliding and soaring through the air, and then, as suddenly as it had appeared, it disappeared.

Now the circled turtles were standing high on their hind legs, stepping away from their shells. I was astounded; I had never seen or heard of a turtle free of its shell, walking like a person.

These turtles without their shells were shaped the way people are without clothes, with two legs and two arms. The main difference was that they had little tails hanging down, and humans don't. I couldn't tell a boy turtle from a girl turtle, although I was sure they could.

Some of the turtles were green and some were greenish-brown with yellow, red or orange markings. They all had dark, mysterious eyes, wide grins and no teeth. Their nostrils looked like two tiny pin holes. Their muscles began at the top of their skulls and gracefully wound their way down into their feet. They looked very old, but they also looked strong. There was not a fat turtle in the group.

In the open air and free of their shells, the turtles stretched high and wide. They looked like dancers preparing for a performance. They mingled and helped one another limber up.

The turtles' gestures were very animated. Without a doubt they were excited about something. They kept pointing to the sky as if they, along with the frogs, were waiting and watching for something, something besides the eagle, but I couldn't tell why or what. Their arms had an unusual way of swimming through the air as they moved.

The center turtle reappeared from inside its shell, also walking on its two hind legs and leaving its shell behind. The two frogs hurried forward on their hind legs to help the center turtle pick up and carry a large bowl of water much too awkward and heavy for the turtle to carry alone -- the poor thing would have looked like a spider trying to carry a particularly large egg.

As careful as the turtle and the two frogs were, water sloshed over the rim of the bowl. The turtle and frogs walked even more slowly so as not to spill any more than they already had. I wondered what the water was for.

Help was coming. Bravo! The other turtles gathered around to offer their support. All together the turtles and the frogs carefully lifted the container of water onto the top of the center turtle's shell-house. I bet they're breathing hard, I thought.

When this task was accomplished, the helping turtles clapped with glee and went back to their places to continue stretching. The frogs returned to their place of watchful waiting.

Although the back legs of the turtles were shorter than their forelimbs, they were still very agile and could move quickly. The center turtle walked around its shell, making certain the bowl was secure. The eagle was nowhere to be seen.

Eventually, the turtles stopped stretching and reached out to one another, to form a perfect circle. Their forelimbs were extended but their prickly nails didn't touch. They waited breathlessly on the tips of their claw-nailed feet. Were they getting ready to dance?

Now the center turtle joined the others. Its action apparently was the signal for the tips of the turtles' prickly nails to touch, and the circle closed in. All the turtles tilted their heads to the left, their heads then swung to the right, and they started to move. Their dance began.

I heard music coming softly toward me as if from worlds away. It was urging the turtles along at a brisk rate.

Step slide. Step slide. Step slide. Step slide.

Periodically, the turtles stopped and wiggled their tails, which made them laugh. It made me laugh, too. The laughter seemed to encourage movement. The faster the wagging, the faster the music.

Step slide. Step slide. Step slide. Step slide.

I never knew turtles could dance. I always thought they were slow and awkward. I was wrong. These turtles, free of their shells, looked like trained dancers, moving with graceful fluidity.

The turtles repeated the gliding step, occasionally touching the earth as if giving it a blessing, and then touching the sky as if they were blessing that, too. They repeated the gliding part, moved in towards the center of the circle and then back out.

Step slide. Step slide. Step slide. Step slide. Pounce! Tails wag and turn about.

I moved the moonstone lower on my forehead. This adjustment changed the picture and brought me closer so I could see better.

The center turtle stepped inside the circle, close to the bowl of water. At the same time, it extended a forelimb up to the sky. The paw-arm was reaching up to where I was watching. The center turtle was reaching for me.

My forehead felt hot, as if the moonstone might go right into the center of my skull. The turtle paw-hand continued to reach toward me. It was as large as my hand, maybe larger. Come on, it seemed to say. Come and join us!

"Do you think I can?" I asked from inside myself. I had never done anything like this before; certainly I had never danced with a turtle.

The center turtle answered by continuing to reach toward me. With a great deal of apprehension and other worried feelings, I reached to grab hold of the wrinkly skin.

We didn't connect. I saw my hand and the turtle paw as they went past each other. I tried my other hand. Still we didn't connect. We were missing each other as if we were in two different galaxies.

There must be a way for me to join the dance, I thought. I challenged my brain to discover how to be closer, to find some sort of opening I could pass through. I went deeper inside myself.

Suddenly, the center turtle rose in the air, gathered my hands in its paws and drew me up. We were flying! Again I was astounded; I never knew turtles could fly.

For a moment, I lost my breath. I was actually in the air above the lake. Only a thin silver cord connected the me in the air with the me on the rock.

I was two me's! One me lay peacefully below, with the moonstone still pressed against my forehead. The flying me worried about falling for about ten seconds. During that short time, I learned to trust the air just as I learned to trust the water when I first learned to swim. I relaxed and breathed with greater ease. The turtle guided me with gentle firmness.

I went flying over Doc's house.

"Can you see me, Doc?" I shouted. "I'm flying!"

I had no idea where I was going, no idea how high I could fly.

I looked forward instead of down so I wouldn't get dizzy. I imagined pictures of the grass and the turtles wagging their little tails. The world about me was beginning to change from sky blue to sky green.

All at once, a lot of turtle paws reached through a big green cloud and cradled me. As they did, my flight slowed down.

These paws were old and leathery, too. I was surprised. I had thought turtles were cool, like snakes and other reptiles. However, these paws were warm, like the door knob in the cottage the night before and my visitor and my moonstone.

I lay back in the turtle paw-arms, and gradually the traveling speed picked up. The wind rushed by my ears the way it does when I stick my head out of a car window. Still, there was something very quiet about what was happening.

And then the flight ended. The air was no longer moving, and I descended gradually through space. For a moment I felt I must have been dropped into the lake, because I was soaking wet. Slowly, everything around me came into focus, as if I had put on special glasses. I noticed there was only one me again; somehow the me on the rock had joined the me in the air.

Much to my surprise, I landed in the middle of a big bowl. It was white and very shiny and clean and filled with water. It wobbled from side to side more precariously than I would have liked. When I stood up, I found the water was up to my neck. I tried to see what was outside the bowl, but I couldn't get my balance enough to get a good look; every time I thought I had it, I fell down.

"Yoo-hoo," I called, "can anyone hear me? Is anyone here? Yoo-hoo!"

No one answered.

"Yoo-hoo! Yoo-hoo!"

I kept falling back into the water. Oh, bother, I thought, how am I going to get out of this? Clearly I couldn't get out by myself.

After several more dunkings, I found my balance in the center of the bowl just long enough to get a good peek over the edge.

By golly! I had found my way back to the turtles after all. I was in the white bowl that was balanced on the center turtle's shell. The turtles down below were dancing around me, as if I were a maypole. They circled and wove in and out among themselves. Step slide, step slide, step slide. But did they know I was there?

"Yoo-hoo! I'm here! Someone. Anyone. I'm stuck. I need your help, or I'll never get out of this bowl!"

I lost my balance again and again, and tumbled under the water time after time. Since I was soaking wet, I weighed a lot more than I usually do. My body felt very cumbersome. I wasn't cold, though. The sun had warmed the water. I wished desperately I could get out and join the turtles.

"Yoo-hoo! Can you hear me?"

I felt like a fish flopping around in a bucket. Water kept going up my nose.

"Yoo-hoo!"

My voice was hoarse from shouting and my body ached from its many falls. I felt like a trapped goldfish. I was so afraid the dance would be over before they noticed me, or before I figured a way out. Fiddlesticks!

"Yoo-hoo!"

Tears of frustration welled up in my eyes. I had come so far and there I was, stuck in a stupid bowl of water.

When they stop dancing, I thought, maybe then they will be able to hear me. I hated being left out.

I looked at my feet. The water in the bowl was so clear and clean I could see each toe. I wondered if there might be some sort of plug I could pull out. My feet began to search the bottom of the bowl as my eyes and hands scanned the sides.

Wait! Were my feet deceiving me? I felt what might be a crack down along the bottom of the bowl! My eyes followed what my feet felt. Was there a tiny door down there? Was there a knob or handle?

I took a deep breath, held my nose, and ducked under the surface of the water. I kept my eyes open as wide as I could until I discovered a very thin crack with my fingers.

Suddenly I started spinning and spiraling. I couldn't stop myself. I must have inadvertently touched something very important, because the water was pouring out of the bowl and I was going right along with it.

Around and around the bowl I went. I was in the center of a whirlpool.

I couldn't think very clearly. I was getting too dizzy. I spun so fast that the world looked like nothing but light.

Abruptly the spinning stopped. I fell heavily on to something very soft. For the longest moment I didn't move. Then I coughed and sputtered to clear the water out of my chest.

As soon as my eyes stopped burning from the water and light, I could see where I was. I found myself sitting in a soft pile of pale green moss. The turtles were still dancing -- they hadn't missed a step. They danced as if nothing had happened.

Water dripped off my hair, my nose, my shoulders. My shirt and pants stuck to my body, heavy and shiny with water.

I wiped the water off my face and the back of my head with my wet hands. Instantly, I was showered with green sparkly lights. I chose to ignore them since my concentration was on the dancing turtles. I felt a little the way I do at school when I am picked last to be on a team.

I decided to take off my outer clothes so I could spread them out on the moss to dry. Wearing heavy clothing didn't feel right, not where I was, not when the turtles weren't wearing anything. The sparkly green lights danced magically around me. I was full of an unusual amount of strength.

I put down the moonstone where I thought it would be safe. I pulled my baggy pants down over my hips. I saw my skin ever so slowly turn a muddy, freckly green. My hands and nails grew long and pointed. The hair on my arms was disappearing and I imagined the nipples on my chest were turning into a dark shade of green. I was becoming one of them! I reminded myself of Doc's words: not to be afraid. This center turtle had to be one of the teachers he had mentioned. Had to be! And the eagle? Maybe the eagle, too.

I totally forgot about the moonstone.

Music surrounded the turtles and me. It was an ensemble of sounds from recorders and other wind instruments, high and hollow. Thank goodness Cassie wasn't there. She doesn't like it when I practice my recorder; she howls more loudly than I can play.

The melody was mesmerizing. The players repeated the same song over and over again, led by a different soloist each time. It went like this:

I couldn't see where the music was coming from. I wondered if I were in one of those old musical movies my mother liked, such as "Singin' In The Rain" where the music emerges magically out of street lamps and bushes. The music was almost as intoxicating as the smell of lavender and rosemary in Doc's garden.

I listened to the music attentively as my body continued to change. I saw blades of grass made up the string section of the orchestra, supporting the reed instruments. The more they rubbed against one another, the richer the sound. As they swayed from side to side,

43

they created their own special part of the song, swinging in perfect harmony.

The cattails behind the frogs had parts, too. They reached deep into their throats for the bass notes. They played the same low notes over and over again.

The weeping willows surrounding the little glen carried the high part. They were the sopranos. I wondered if what I heard were their tears. Their sound tinkled like the glass mobile in the kitchen of our city house. The willows shimmered as they sang.

Then, I saw a little foot path leading down from the moss mound to where the dancing was. It was made of woven balsam boughs, one bough knotted to another. I was sure the path was made for me.

I stood up in my new skin and stepped onto the balsam path. I walked very carefully from bough to bough. When I reached the end of the path, I gently put my turtle-like feet down on the soft grass the turtles were dancing upon. It felt spongier than the softest of living room rugs.

I wanted to dance with the turtles. I opened my arms. I felt the earth hum with life as I looked for an opening.

Step slide. Step slide. Step and slide. Pounce!

The vibrations moving through the soles of my turtle-like feet made me ache to enter the circle.

Touch the sky. Touch the earth. Turn yourself about!

At first, the turtles wouldn't stop dancing to let me join them -- or even say hello, for that matter. I sensed they might not know I was there. So I waited. I kept my arms outstretched, hoping one of the turtles would beckon me in.

All at once, with an energy that must have come from the sun, my body spun around, my head tilted to the left, then swung to the right, and I was absorbed into the circle. Without being told to begin, I found myself dancing.

I had never danced so fast! I was surprised I could keep up. Learning new dance steps was never easy for me when I was in school. This was different. I was learning the dance steps like a professional dancer.

Step and slide. Step and slide. Step and slide.

At that moment, my body knew it all. My body and my mind joined together perfectly in a mystical way. Rather than thinking which foot went where, I just did it.

Step and slide. Step and slide. Step and slide.

As I danced, I was filled with joy, as if I were floating. I was used to feeling clumsy and oafish -- the worst one in my ballet class -- but not now.

Oh my, the dance was just as much fun as I thought it would be. I was leading at the same time I was being led. I was one with the turtles. The feeling of excitement and freedom I felt was better than being on a Ferris wheel, better than going sledding down a steep and slick hill, even better than sailing. I never thought I would ever feel anything was better than sailing.

Around and around and around we went, sometimes faster, sometimes slower. Always it was the same basic step -- step and slide, step and slide -- but each round was a little different. We dancers were creating our own dance as we went, and the dance was creating its own form.

The grasses continued to play, the weeping willows and the cattails continued to sing. I no longer could tell the dancers from the dance, the players from the song.

I wished I knew or could hear the words to the song, but I couldn't. I could see the turtles singing them -- I could see it in their eyes, I could sense it in their breathing.

The words simply escaped my ears, so I hummed along the best I could because I was happy, happier than I had ever been in my life. I knew full well that my humming wasn't the same as what they were singing, but it didn't matter.

Step slide. Step slide. Run high to the sun and back to the earth!

All at once, without any warning I could see or feel, the turtles stopped circling and dancing. They dropped their arms and ran to the green mossy dell, where I saw them pick up a small stone. It was my moonstone!

They were delighted with it, and began jumping up and down, wagging their tails, clapping their claws and tossing the moonstone high in the air.

The noise they made with their forelimbs and feet was deafening. They sounded like an army of squirrels running across the tin roof of the boat shed. I waved my arms frantically, hoping to get their attention. They didn't seem to understand the moonstone was mine. I wanted it back.

I did my best to stop dancing, but I couldn't pull myself away from the step and slide cadence. The more I tried, the more my body insisted I continue to move in the circle -- over and over, round and round, all by myself.

Step and slide. Step and slide. Turn, bless the earth, acknowledge the sky!

The turtles continued clapping, wagging and jumping. The moonstone shone as if it had a life of its own. The louder the turtles got, the more strength I received for my dance. In fact, I couldn't contain what they were giving me. The strength pushed me away from the ground, still attached to my silver cord.

"No," I yelled. 'I can't go. Not yet. I don't have my moonstone!"

My legs moved faster and faster. I was dancing over the heads of the turtles. The air moved quickly around my face -- I recognized the sensation. I knew I couldn't stop.

As the turtles' clapping and pounding intensified, I went higher. The higher I went, the smaller everything else became -- the turtles, the trees, the rock, the frogs, the cattails, too. I looked down, and felt a stab of frustration. I didn't want to leave my moonstone, my treasure, behind.

Suddenly I noticed the center turtle was standing in the middle of the clapping and stamping turtles again. The center turtle appeared to be changing its form into something red and black. I saw jeans and a lumberjack's boots. The form bent down and picked up something -- I was sure it was my moonstone.

"Hey!" I shouted. "It's mine! Hey, I know who you are! Bring me back! Bring me back down! Now! You have some explaining to do. What's going on?"

No one heard me. I went higher and higher.

That was when I became afraid. And as soon as I became afraid, my flight was over. My silver cord was tugging me down.

"Don't drop me," I yelled.

The air rushed forcefully past my ears. My fingers and toes tingled as if all the blood in my body were being pulled out. I heard myself shouting, but my voice grew distant and muffled. I closed my eyes.

Then, everything was quiet -- everything except the sound of water lapping against the back rock, water gently rippling close to my feet.

I knew the turtles were gone, even though my eyes were still closed.

Cassie nudged me with her nose.

I must be back at the lake, I thought, back in my body.

Slowly I opened my eyes. I was on the green mossy mound. I saw two blue orbs of light -- Cassie's nose was three inches from my face and her cool, ice blue eyes were looking directly at me. She tried to lick not just my lips, but the inside of my mouth. She does that when she needs to know where I've been.

I stuck my hands and feet up in the air and looked at my fingers and toes. My skin was white and freckly. No more green. No more claws. No more wrinkly skin.

I suddenly remembered my moonstone. Frantically I searched the mound. I found nothing.

I stood up slowly and walked almost dream-like toward the cottage, glad to be back on firm ground. I had no idea where my moonstone was. Furthermore, what did the lumberjack want with it? And what was the connection between the lumberjack and the turtles?

Everything was getting more complicated rather than less so. My poor brain! My poor, poor brain!

My heart raced as I thought about my missing moonstone and all my recent adventures. I felt I had just awakened from a journey to the center of life. I couldn't wait to talk to Doc.

CHAPTER THREE

Later that day I paddled down the lake to tell Doc about all that had happened. He listened intently and then smiled when I told him about the disappearance of my mysterious moonstone and the turtles. He didn't seem either worried or concerned. In fact, he was rather amused.

"Why don't you make a pouch for your moonstone and wear it around your neck?" suggested Doc. "That way, when it comes back into your life, as it is bound to do, you won't lose it or misplace it. And I'll put a lock on your cottage door tomorrow."

"I didn't lose the moonstone," I said defensively. "It disappeared. That's different! Maybe it was stolen. Did you ever think of that?"

"Whatever," said Doc.

"What kind of pouch?" I asked. "You mean a small satchel?"

"Yes," he replied. "Long ago people wore pouches around their necks to carry their lucky stones and good luck charms, their amulets. The moonstone has special power. You don't want it to disappear again, do you?"

"No, I don't."

"Wearing the moonstone around your neck will help you feel more from your heart -- you know, instead of thinking and worrying so much about being either naughty or judged by God. The moonstone will help you feel you are perfect exactly the way you are. You don't need to please anyone else."

He's right, I thought to myself. I do spend an inordinate amount of time trying to please my parents, people at school. That's why I work so hard to get good grades and do what I'm told. But how did Doc know that? Moonstones couldn't have that kind of power.

When I got back to the cottage, I did as Doc suggested and made a pouch out of a small piece of leather and a braided string of hemp. Who knew where the moonstone was at that moment, but I was going to be ready in the event I ever found it again. I still hadn't figured out how it got from the house to the bottom of the lake or what the turtles and the lumberjack were doing with it now. Doc said I asked too many questions. All I wanted was a few answers. I didn't think I was asking too much.

I thought about the moonstone a lot, hoping the turtles would drop it back into my world. Should I, could I, go back for it?

*

By three days after the big storm, I was really annoyed. I had no idea where the moonstone was. My new friends should have come back. The turtles had not returned to give me another ride. I hadn't seen another eagle, and they usually fly above the lake all the time. Doc said I had been given an out-of-body experience. Who knew?

On the days I meditated at the back rock, instead of seeing turtles, I saw colors moving -- no pictures, just shapes. I longed to go back to continue the dance, learn the words to the song, and reclaim my moonstone, but I didn't know how to do any of those things. Maybe it was just as well. But I surely missed the moonstone. I loved the way it made me feel.

One evening while it was still light, I paddled down the lake to see Doc again. I knew he'd be home. That's the nature of a hermit.

"I need to see the turtles again," I said desperately. "You must help me. I'm running out of time. My parents may be back any day now!"

"You can't make this kind of experience happen," Doc said. "You were given a gift the day you went flying. I told you not to be afraid, but apparently you were. How the stranger fits in, I don't know. All I can suggest is that you be ready to receive anyone you think is a teacher or guide with an open heart. However, if the stranger comes back and you feel either afraid or unsafe, make certain the lock I put on your door is secured and in a fierce voice say 'Go away!' Follow your instinct. You're a sensible lass."

I could feel myself scowling. I sensed Doc wasn't altogether comfortable about who the stranger was. But he loved the part about the turtles.

Making myself ready and opening my heart to receive a teacher sounded a little vague to me. I wanted an explicit instruction, such as I should light three candles, or sing my school song at the top of my lungs, or rub two sticks together, or light a smudge pot in the backyard.

Was that asking too much?

When I returned home, I paddled to our dock in the back bay. Another precious day had passed, and again nothing happened. I liked having a lock on the cottage door.

I tied up the canoe and looked to the west, wondering if there was another storm on the horizon. I saw nothing but a beautiful sunset. I lay face down on the dock and looked between the planks. I hoped to see the dock's resident snapping turtle -- that's how badly I wanted to see a turtle. The snapping turtle had lived under the dock for at least as long as I had been alive.

Nothing. All I saw was my reflection, glowing like the sky as the sun finished its day in a blaze of reds, yellows and oranges. It was quiet everywhere.

Cassie came down to the dock to escort me back to the cottage. As we walked toward the bay side door, I took one last look into the woods, hoping a turtle would appear on the path.

Periodically in my imagination, I saw my strange visitor of a few nights before coming toward me, but he did not materialize. I reminded myself not to be afraid if he came again. After all, he was just the center turtle in disguise. He was the one who had the power to take me to the turtle green. I wondered if my skin would change a second time.

I found it very dark inside the cottage. Through the front window, I watched the last trace of red in the sky disappear. The lake was serene. I lit two kerosene lamps, and built a fire to warm my bones. Then I sat down with my tapestry and continued my project.

I worked with a lot of green that night, then yellow, then back to green again. The green and the yellow had to go together. Sometimes when I was in Doc's garden, greens and yellows were the only colors I saw.

I felt like a lovesick puppy, longing for the turtles the way I did. I told myself my longing was useless. I kept wishing for a knock, anyway. The only noises I heard came from the fire. Then:

"Me-e-ow!"

There was no mistaking that cry. It was Twyla.

Twyla only gave three-syllable cries to be let in when she had a gift for me. So I put my tapestry down and hurried to the door. I unlocked it and Twyla darted in, her mouth full with a sweet young deer mouse.

"No, Twyla, not inside! Your mouse is still alive!"

Twyla pretended she didn't hear me. She, like Cassie, only listened to me when she felt like it. Instead of going back out, she put her prize down at my feet. She wanted praise.

The mouse squeaked. I left the door open, hoping the mouse would scurry out and the turtles would scurry in. Unfortunately, a battalion of mosquitoes came charging in, attracted to the light. I had no choice but to close the door and shut the mouse in. The poor mouse was frozen with fear.

I knelt down to see it better.

"Hello, pretty thing!"

I caught myself acting just as weirdly as Doc by talking to the mouse. I was glad my parents weren't there to tease me.

"How are you tonight?"

I didn't expect the mouse to answer, so I watched it carefully to see what it would do. This deer mouse was an exquisite creature. It had a white underside just like Cassie's.

The mouse, Twyla, and I stayed motionless, watching one another for a long time. When the room was finally quiet enough, the mouse started to tiptoe away.

"No!" Twyla meowed angrily, knocking the poor deer mouse onto its side with her front paw. "You stay!"

I stood up to watch Twyla discipline the mouse. The poor mouse was squeaking in fright. Twyla pushed it over backward again and again, each time it showed a sign of life. Finally, the mouse lay still, looking dead. Twyla wasn't fooled. She remained ready to pounce.

"Come on, little mouse, don't give up now -- Twy will eat you." I touched it gently with one of my toes.

"Squeak!" bellowed the small mouse in its biggest voice. It gathered its hind legs under itself and sat back up. I frightened it more than the cat did.

Twyla softened, looked away and appeared to be thinking about something else. Small mouse knew as well as I did that Twyla had eyes at the end of her tail. The cat rubbed around my ankles and purred.

When the mouse was convinced Twyla was bored with the hunt, it fearfully tried one last time to tiptoe away as quietly and inconspicuously as it could. It looked like Jerry, the cartoon mouse, sneaking away from Tom.

"No!" meowed Twyla, jumping quickly away from me and back toward the mouse. Once more she tossed the poor little thing into the air. The mouse could no longer squeak. I smelled its fear and saw its little heart beating rapidly under its white fur.

The small mouse made itself even smaller as it tried to disappear into one of the ridges of the blue braided rug. Twyla reminded me of me during one of my training sessions with Cassie. Does Twyla remember? "Sit. Stay. Down."

Twyla climbed up on the red pillow by the fire. She was Queen Twyla, ruler of mice, sitting on a goose down throne. She curled up into a ball and closed her yellow eyes half way. Her tail whipped from side to side.

The young mouse wriggled its nose as it tried to decide what to do next. It was in a quandary. Watchful waiting wasn't doing it much good.

"Don't move, small one," I said. "The Queen is not asleep." I was worried Twyla would pounce and scold the mouse to death.

The poor deer mouse looked so tired. It was worried, worried sick. It stayed obediently in the middle of the rug, waiting, watching every movement.

I was the one who finally took action.

"Enough!" I announced. "This mouse goes out!"

Twyla jumped down from her throne and sat protectively by her prize. The mouse was so weary it didn't even flinch at having the cat so close. I reached in the garbage bag for an empty dog food can.

I walked as quietly as I could to the mouse and put the can over its head and scooped it up. Catching it was easy.

"Me-e-ow-ow!"

This time Twyla's cry had four syllables.

I went to the door, opened it and let the mouse out of the can under the porch. At first it sat without moving, watching, waiting, but then it hurried under the wood pile.

When I went back inside, I saw Twyla with her tail held high, going around the corner of the living room into the bedroom. I had hurt her feelings.

It was 11 PM. Another day gone and soon another night. No visitor -- unless I called the mouse a visitor. No turtles. For awhile, Twyla and the mouse had helped me forget about "getting ready" and "opening my heart." I took one final look around the cottage and relocked the door.

As I prepared for bed and thought about the day to come, I became a little more optimistic. I blew out the lamps and headed toward the bedroom.

The night was bright -- as sparkly and clear as the day had been. I found my way to the bed by moonlight rather than flashlight. When I settled under the covers, I looked out to say goodnight to the world.

The moon was radiant and full. I liked seeing her in her glory. I arranged my pillows against the window sill and leaned back to watch her reflection on the lake before I went to sleep. I didn't see Twyla anywhere.

The moon is my friend, the caretaker of the people I love. On that night, I felt very close to Granny Rose and my parents, knowing the moon was shining on them, as well.

The higher the moon climbed in the sky, the more her light splashed over my face. I felt her cool glow on my cheeks.

There was so much light in the room I knew I could read a book without a flashlight. I wondered how the moon would look through the moonstone. I knew it would be bright. The moon's light shone so brightly my eyes watered. It was more powerful than usual.

I wiped my eyes with the sheet. The light was everywhere and I knew the moon wasn't the only source. The room got brighter and brighter. This time, though, it wasn't just my eyes that felt the light -- it was my whole body.

I looked up to the ceiling to see if I could see where the extra light was coming from. It was too bright to do even that. My eyes kept watering.

"Yoo-hoo!"

I heard what sounded like the voice of Granny Rose.

"Yip-ee!" I shouted involuntarily. I wasn't a single bit afraid.

I sat up and wiped my watering eyes. The light continued expanding.

"Yoo-hoo!" I heard again. "Yoo-hoo!"

I hastily grabbed my flashlight -- out of habit, I suppose, because I certainly didn't need it -- and swung my legs off the side of the bed.

"Stay where you are," the voice said. "I'm coming to you!"

My heart pounded. The voice might sound like Granny Rose, but in no way could it be Granny Rose. I put my flashlight down. The voice was all around me, as well as inside me, the way it had been the night of the storm.

"Come in!" I said out loud. "I'm here. I've been hoping someone would come."

The light in the room was so bright, the moon looked dull by comparison. A golden dome created itself at the foot of my bed. Then it became a curious mixture of gold and green flecks. I remembered the light tumbling around me when my skin turned green with the turtles.

All at once, a woman emerged out of the glow. She stood in the doorway. She looked like Granny Rose, so of course I wasn't afraid. She looked at me and I looked at her. She smiled, but I frowned. No one could look like Granny Rose except Granny Rose, but she was in the hospital. How did this woman get in? I had locked the door. I came to the conclusion my guest was a Granny Rose look alike.

Suddenly a wave of disappointment rushed over me. I had prayed for a turtle. I wanted my moonstone back. It was hard to smile when all I got was a little old lady.

My visitor was old, slightly overweight but comfortably soft. She wore a green polyester pantsuit, like the one Granny Rose wore each time she came for a visit. The visitor had short, gray, curly hair that framed her face and great brown eyes. Her lips, her teeth, her eyes all shone.

I planned to say, "Hello, I'm glad you've come," But instead, I heard myself say: "Where are the turtles?"

My guest was as surprised as I was. She thought a moment, assumed a knowing look and said:

"Oh, dearie me, I have offended you. I have worn the wrong thing. I am really not used to all this traveling."

Her voice was high and shrill, sounding like mine when I'm feeling frantic.

"No, no," I said hastily, "you look fine. Really you do. I was expecting someone else, that's all. I'm sorry I was rude."

"Oh, I understand," she replied. "Perhaps you would be more comfortable if I changed and became someone or something else. Would you please help me with my zipper?"

The old woman turned around and presented her back to me.

"I find these suits terribly hard to get in and out of."

I looked up and down her back, but I saw no zipper. All I saw was a big oversized sweater she was wearing on top of a pantsuit. Under the sweater was a vest and under the vest was one of my father's old short-sleeved shirts -- like the one I wore frequently at the lake. On her feet were white nurses' shoes and white anklets.

The woman must have borrowed her clothes from people I knew. All the clothes looked vaguely familiar. Her hands kept fumbling around in her hair.

"Excuse me," I said, "but zippers don't start in the hair. Zippers start at the neck, or at the waist."

"Oh yes, of course!"

The old woman kept her hands where they were, fumbling and searching. I didn't know what else to say. I didn't even see a center seam where a zipper might be.

The woman's frustration increased until I worried she might cry.

"Ma'am, you look fine the way you are. Don't worry about a silly old zipper," I said.

"Of course I worry. I do not want to stay looking like this forever and ever."

For a moment, neither of us said anything. Then I saw what I should have seen all along. The green polyester pantsuit and the shirt and the sweater and the shoes were all of a piece. There wasn't a seam or a placket anywhere; everything was painted on.

I looked down at her shoes and saw a little dirt painted there. I also saw a coffee stain on the front of her vest.

"Turn around again," I said. "Let me take another look." I decided the old woman knew what she was doing.

This time I put my hand onto the woman's head, thinking if I couldn't see a zipper, perhaps I might feel one.

Without pulling or pushing or any other zipper-like movement, her body began to change. I felt heat and strength pour over me from the end of the bed. The feeling rushed through my arm. The golden light around her changed. There were all kinds of little green flecks moving in and out, shiny and bright like wet grass.

An opening appeared down the center of her back. Before I could see what was underneath the green pantsuit, she turned around.

What a wonderful smile she had for me! Her eyes had a mischievous twinkle and her two dimples deepened. Gradually, a man's face began to appear beneath the smile! The smile never changed.

"Good grief," I gasped. "How did you do that?"

Standing before me was a man dressed in a three-piece business suit, the kind my father wore to work. The man had long, flowing white hair that was braided, with three feathers on his head -- one yellow, one green and one red. He looked as if he were a native Canadian Indian ready to do business at the local bank. He spoke before I had a chance to question him.

"There now, is this better? Do you like my feathers?"

"I suppose so," I answered. "Although you've got me so mixed up right now, I don't know what I like or what I think."

I saw stripes painted on his tie and veins painted on the back of his hands. Maybe he's a ghost after all, I thought. Maybe he's related to the lumberjack.

"You know," he said, "if I came looking like the ghost maiden your father described to you, you would not have anything to do with me. You would be too frightened and I would go away."

I remained silent and kept staring. How did he know about the ghost maiden? I had never told anyone about her.

All the fuss about clothes confused me. I didn't care what my visitor wore. I wanted to know where he came from, and how he got to the lake and into my bedroom. I wanted him to stay a good long time so he could explain everything. I was getting used to the unpredictable nature of my visitors.

"My staying depends upon you," he said. "I will stay as long as you are neither frightened nor sleepy."

My guest once again spoke arhythmically, choosing and enunciating his words very carefully.

"I'm not sleepy. I'm not afraid," I said, looking directly into his painted eyes.

"Well, you must have been afraid of something when I came before, because you literally blew me, the lumberjack, out of sight and out the door."

What? He was the lumberjack? Could it be? What did he mean when he said I blew the lumberjack out the door? The lumberjack simply disappeared. Then I remembered. I had been afraid! I was afraid of the dumb spider in the teapot. I stepped on it and killed it, which was exactly when the lumberjack disappeared.

"Spiders are not dumb," my guest said seriously. He read my thoughts again. "Come, help me one more time so you may be more comfortable with me."

Well, I thought as I shook my head from side to side, the lumberjack was more of a magician than a weird-o.

As the lumberjack walked over to me and turned around, I knew what to do. I put my hand on the back of his head and imagined there was a zipper there. The three-piece suit gradually changed into the outfit of my visitor on the night of the storm, except this time the colors of his clothes were all the colors I was putting into my tapestry. The lumberjack turned and faced me. He spoke while the change was taking place.

"Let me introduce myself. My name is Aaron. But wait."

Suddenly the lumberjack disappeared. As before, the colors rearranged themselves before my eyes. When the lights stopped shifting and changing, a different but familiar creature stood before me.

"Oh my," I gasped. "You! You're the center turtle. You are amazing!"

The turtle turned around on one leg and bowed.

"Who are you, anyway?" I exclaimed. "I mean, what or who are you really?"

The creature scratched his turtle head with his pointed claw-nails. He blinked each time he spoke.

"I am Aaron. Right now, I am a turtle because you expected a turtle," he said. "As you noticed, I can be anything. I simply think myself into what I think you need me to be so you don't chase me away with fear."

Aaron rubbed his skin briskly with his rough fore-claws.

"Do you have a last name?" I asked.

"Negative. Aaron is my only name. I must say though, you are spelling my name wrong in your thoughts. It is Aron, one a, not two."

"A-r-o-n?" I repeated.

"Precisely!"

Aron sat down on the edge of the bed. The closer he came, the greater his warmth. The night was cold, but I was so warm I could sit up without a robe or covers.

Aron had trouble sitting still. He was fidgeting the way I used to when I had my picture taken. He stood and paced about the foot of the bed, looking as if he would rather be dancing. I saw his turtle skin was painted on, too.

"Where I come from, we do not have bodies like you," Aron said. "A body is a wonderful thing when you are on earth, but it is a bit cumbersome for me when I travel in spirit as much as I do. So I travel light!"

"Where do you come from?" I asked.

Aron pointed up to the sky, spun around and pointed over the lake, jumped three times and pointed down under the bed. He shrugged. His whole body spoke as he searched for his words.

"You see, I am your U.P.," Aron said.

I knew he knew I didn't understand.

"Your Universal Parent," he said. "Everyone has one. I am a part of you. You are a part of me."

"Then it was you who came in the storm?" I asked.

"Precisely!" he said.

"Was it you dancing on the green?"

"Precisely!"

"Was it you in the green polyester pantsuit?" I persisted.

"Precisely!"

Aron spoke through his wide turtle mouth, which looked like a great black hole -- no teeth, no pink gums. My father never told me about anything like this when he told me ghost stories.

"For goodness sake, stop thinking I am a ghost," Aron said with irritation. "You do not see me going around saying boo and scaring people, do you? I am here tonight to teach you about listening."

I looked into Aron's eyes, and he began to hum. This tune, like the turtles' song, was short and easy to remember. He hummed it over and over again.

Soon, Aron's humming tuned into singing.

I studied his face, tilting from side to side as he sang. His eye sockets looked as black as his mouth. Each time he took a breath, I saw a bony ridge, where teeth would have been had he been human.

I decided to sing along with him. My voice, the one I heard coming from my lips, sounded tinny compared to his that also came from inside me. I picked up the song easily.

THERE'S A LIGHT A - ROUND ME,

A loon joined in from the lake outside my window.

GUID-ING ME. TO SEE.

The loon was joined by a bull frog and a few crickets.

NOW THE LIGHT'S WITH - IN ME,

Twyla jumped up onto the window ledge next to the bed and sang, too. The pine trees hummed with whispering voices and Cassie climbed out from under the bed and howled.

TEACH -ING ME TO BE.

The whole lake was getting brighter and lighter because we were all singing the same song.

68

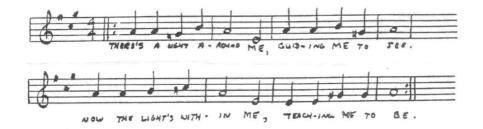

THERE'S A LIGHT A-ROUND ME, GUID-ING ME TO SEE.

NOW THE LIGHT'S WITH-IN ME, TEACH-ING ME TO BE.

Suddenly, as if we shared the same conductor, we all stopped. I looked at Aron. It was so quiet I thought I could hear the moon.

"That was wonderful," I said. "I never knew all the wood creatures, the moon, the trees, could sing!"

"When you learn to tune in your ears and quiet your mind," said Aron, "you'll discover you are surrounded by music all the time."

I wanted to hear more about the music. However, my need to ask questions continued to guide the conversation.

"Doc said I should expect a teacher or a guide. Was he right?"

"Precisely!" Aron answered. "I heard you wanted a teacher to remind you of things you already knew but had forgotten."

Aron was right.

"You didn't call by yelling 'yoo-hoo'. You called by being ready."

Now Aron was sounding like Doc.

The turtle hopped on and off the bed as nimbly as any dancer or gymnast I had ever seen. He stretched up toward the ceiling, turned around, and sat down again. He knew I was thinking hard. He waited for me to absorb his words.

"I don't feel very ready right now," I said. "In fact, I'm feeling pretty stupid. I feel the way I did when I did poorly on an I.Q. test a couple of years ago. I didn't know what the questions were asking."

"You will, when you learn to believe in yourself and, of course, open your heart."

"Open my heart? How do I do that?" I asked.

Aron shrugged. "You'll know." He extended one leg high to the side, put it back down, and then did the same thing with the other leg. "The first thing you must learn is to recognize your teachers. They surround you. Right here. Right this very minute."

I looked around. All I saw was Cassie.

"Precisely!" Aron said. "She is a teacher, and a very patient one at that."

"You must be crazy!" I said. "Cassie's just a dog."

"No one or no thing is ever just an anything," Aron said firmly.

"But dogs are . . .well, just dogs," I repeated lamely. Aron stopped moving.

"The dog is as much a part of the Universe as you are," Aron said. "Until you can see that and feel that, you won't be able to learn all she has to teach you."

"Cassie a teacher?" I exclaimed. "But I'm the one who is teaching her. I'm teaching her to sit, stay, come. Remember?"

Cassie leaned against one of Aron's turtle legs. If Aron was right, and I sensed he was, then Cassie probably already knew the kind of learning he was telling me about.

"You need to practice listening," Aron insisted. "For instance, who did the singing a few moments ago?"

"You, me, a bull frog, a loon, the pine trees…." I murmured.

"Ah, there you are!" the turtle said, jumping excitedly up and down. "You have just acknowledged many of your teachers of this evening."

"The pine trees, the bull frogs, the loons -- are they teachers, too?"

"Precisely!" Aron replied. "Along with all other living things. Look out the windows and wave at one of the best teachers there is."

"My moon, my dear moon?" I asked.

"Precisely! She is your dear moon in more ways than you know."

I waved, and to my astonishment, the moon blinked at me.

"She blinked!" I cried excitedly.

Aron laughed by hissing between his gums. The hiss sounded as if he were trying to bark.

"Precisely!" he said, smiling his toothless grin. "Moons do that!"

"Is Twyla a teacher, too?"

"Precisely!" Aron said. "She was conducting school in the middle of your living room just a little while ago."

"You mean, when she brought in the deer mouse?"

"Precisely!"

My thoughts returned to Twyla and her mouse. I was baffled. While I gathered my thoughts, Cassie jumped onto the bed, bored, I supposed, by my slowness.

Aron patted Cassie on the head and then bent down and touched his own toes. His movements said as much, if not more, than his words.

"Why don't you practice listening in a new way?" Aron asked. "Stop listening for the answer you want and start listening for the answer that is."

Aron dropped into a split leg position, like a cheerleader, alongside my bed.

"I didn't learn anything from either Twyla or the deer mouse," I said mournfully.

Aron the turtle swung onto his hind feet.

"Sometimes it helps to try to become the teacher who is teaching you. For example, did you look at the mouse through the eyes of the cat? Did you look at the cat through the eyes of the mouse? No, they were just a cat and just a mouse to you."

Aron was right. I only saw Twyla and the mouse through my eyes. But I was concentrating.

"You need to concentrate differently," Aron said. "Go inside yourself as you did when you joined us for the dance on the green. From inside, you can see the teachers around you. Then I won't have to come barging in, surprising you this way."

"I could get used to having you here," I said. "You certainly are a great source of information, information I need. And I thank you for that," I said gratefully.

"It simply makes much more sense for you to learn from earth teachers instead of from me," Aron said. "Do you not agree?"

"Even spiders?" I interjected.

"Especially spiders!" Aron said.

I looked at Aron disbelievingly.

Aron blinked his eyes and started humming. While he hummed, he moved his claw-fingers like a spider going up the water spout.

Then his fingers looked like rain coming down.

The spider fingers climbed up again.

Aron touched my knee. He finished the little tune but went on humming.

Suddenly sleep enveloped me, like a big blue fleecy cloud. I tried to hold it back, but no matter how hard I tried, I couldn't do it. Finally, I gave in to a great big yawn.

Aron sang more softly. I felt he was planning to leave, even though I wanted him to stay. Unfortunately, I was too sleepy to protest. My eye lids were very heavy. The cloud over me darkened to a deep blue, and Aron's singing moved farther and farther away.

"Please don't go," I murmured. "I'm just a little tired -- not much! Please tell me where you left my moonstone."

"You sleep now," Aron answered, ending his song. "We shall meet again."

"Before you go, please, please sing me the turtle song," I pleaded. "You remember, the one you and the other turtles sang on the green, the one you were just humming. I want to learn the words."

I couldn't see Aron anymore. I felt as if I were slipping away, the way I did when I went under anesthesia when I had my tonsils out.

"You can't hear the words because your heart is closed," Aron said quietly.

A new sensation broke forth in me with those words. A different voice was speaking now, a greater voice, neither male nor female. The whole room vibrated.

"Your heart is closed because you hold fear."

I hugged my pillow to keep from being frightened.

"The only way to release fear is by letting in love. Love allows the soul to sing. When you love yourself, you will be able to love all things. Then, and only then, will you know the words to the song. Your teachers will help you remember."

I was feeling too disoriented to answer back. I thought of the spider. I thought of all spiders I had stepped on, all my teachers, oh, my . . . .

"Look into the eyes of the spiders, the frogs, the turtles, the flies. . ." the voice commanded.

All those words about opening the heart and love had me so befuddled. Lizzie jumped up on to the bed and perched over my heart, purring loudly. I faded into the blue space between wakefulness and a deep sleep.

I waved to the moon and thanked her for her steadfastness, for not leaving. She accepted me, even when my heart was closed.

It was cold. Lizzie and I burrowed down as deeply as we could under the rough camp blankets. I missed the light and its warmth.

The song said the light was within me. But where? How was I supposed to find it? I didn't like being cold. I didn't like being only partially informed. I didn't like killing spiders and being afraid of a ghost maiden. And since when had I closed my heart?

I stayed in the blue space as long as I needed to. I thought about the small deer mouse and Twyla. I saw turtles dancing in the palm of my hand. The moon was now my moonstone, hanging from a pine tree rather than resting in my pouch. The moon/moonstone got larger, until the turtles were dancing on the eye of the moon.

Too much. Too fast. I couldn't absorb any more. The pictures and even the colors faded from my consciousness. I slept.

CHAPTER FOUR

"Good morning, world!"
I woke up with a shout.

I don't do that very often, but on that morning I did -- I actually burst into wakefulness. No pause to think about my dreams, no pause in that delicious blue space between being awake and being asleep.

Instead, BANG! I was up and at 'em. I wanted to get the day started. It felt bizarre to say, but I had a teacher to find. And I was determined to find the dancing turtles so I could reclaim that wonderful euphoric feeling of rapture I had when I danced with them on the green. Who knew, maybe I'd get my moonstone back.

I hurriedly fed the cats, went to the outhouse, ate a couple of cookies and gulped down a glass of apple juice. I didn't make my bed. I did bring in more firewood, and I put my dirty glass in the sink with all the other dirty dishes I was accumulating. I wasn't very good at eating right or doing chores when my parents were away. I was planning to take care of that dreary stuff the next day, just like Scarlet O'Hara. Tomorrow. Always tomorrow.

When I did everything I felt I absolutely had to do, I stood in the middle of the living room with my hands on my waist and said to the cats, "Okay, my furry friends, what are you going to teach me today?" Twyla answered by walking to the door -- her signal she wanted to be let out.

I looked at Lizzie. She was cleaning herself after her morning meal. Both cats were busy and preoccupied.

"Ha!" I said under my breath. "Indifferent cats."

"Cassie, Cassie come!" I called.

Cassie jumped off the bed, wagging her tail. She, too, went directly to the door.

"Cassie, what do you have to teach me today?"

Cassie paid no attention to me.

"Drat! Thankless dog!"

I opened the door, and my first three prospective teachers disappeared into the woods. This is going to be harder than I thought, I said to myself.

As I stood in the doorway, I brought my hand to my throat and rubbed the empty pouch. I was glad the pouch was still there, even though it was empty. Maybe I should go to the back rock and wade in the muck in case the moonstone had returned to familiar territory.

Could a moonstone be a teacher, too? I hated thinking I might be missing a learning opportunity.

No, the moonstone couldn't be a teacher, I thought. Aron said to learn from living things -- the frog, the turtle, the water lily -- even spiders, although I couldn't imagine how. Only one thing I knew to be true: I desperately wanted to find my moonstone.

I closed the door, picked up my spider web-swinging stick, and hurried down to the dock so I could look around and see what was happening there. The dock was usually a busy place in the morning, teeming with life -- water bugs, water lilies, bumble bees, dragonflies, turtles, maybe an eagle or two -- a fine collection of teachers. But on this morning, everything was still.

I looked and looked for the turtles. I knew they were somewhere nearby, even when I couldn't see them. Why aren't they surfacing to teach me? I asked myself. It shouldn't be hard to find a teacher if they truly are around me.

I decided to go to the back rock. If I were a teacher, I'd wait for me there.

I charged down the trail, not looking left or right, swinging my spider stick forward and back as if I were leading a patrol of soldiers, breaking all of the spiders' night webs and any other spider web I could see.

When I got to the back rock, I looked around. Again I found nothing but stillness. I thought at least I'd find a frog waiting for me. No such luck. All I saw were ?

lot of big ants scurrying, working, carrying heavy loads into the woods.

Aron hadn't mentioned ants. Good! Ants work too hard. Who wanted a teacher to learn about work? After all, I was on vacation. I wished I had stayed in bed and slept a little longer.

I left the back rock and turned in the direction of the cottage. I moved so quickly I didn't notice the sun, the lake, or the brisk morning wind. I didn't notice the butterflies, the trees, the morning dew. I saw nothing.

In my hurry, I carelessly tripped over a stone, a stone I had walked around my whole life. I fell, and banged my right knee on a pine root.

"Pooh!" I shouted out loud. "Pooh! Pooh! Pooh!"

I felt terrible. My knee throbbed with pain and my frustration was blinding. I couldn't find any teachers anywhere. Could it be Aron was playing a joke on me? Maybe so.

I stayed sprawled in the middle of the narrow path, rubbing my knee, my poor aching knee. I wanted to cry, but no tears came. I wiped my dripping nose on my shirt sleeve. My knee hurt too much to move.

I gave my weight to the earth. I took some deep breaths and felt my breathing slow down. Gradually, my knee began to feel better. The quieter I became, the more I felt the earth sigh.

A fly landed on my arm.

Drat that fly for disturbing me! Now, of all times.

I swatted at it. Missed. It flew away.

Five minutes went by, and I quieted myself again. I looked up into the trees. I saw them sway and circle as they reached for the sun. They looked majestic. The world I saw lying down was much different from the world I saw standing up.

The fly came back. It landed on my arm a second time, on the very same place.

Drat! Again that blasted fly interrupted my thinking.

Again I swatted at it. Again I missed.

I swatted at it one more time.

I missed again. This time my arm stung from my blow. I lay down to continue my reverie. I decided to ignore the fly.

I wondered what Toronto would look like from this position. I tried to imagine lying down on the sidewalk, looking up at the buildings and all the people.

Again the fly landed on my arm.

Again I cursed and tried to kill it.

Again I missed.

And again.

And again.

Each time I tried to kill the fly, I got more annoyed -- hitting harder and harder until my arm was bright red. My arm hurt more than my knee.

The fly came again. It started making quick circles around and around my nose, and then settled on a mole on my arm.

I didn't swat at it. Instead, I slowly sat up and asked: "Okay, fly, what do you want?"

I looked at the fly and the fly looked at me. Each of us was eyeball to eyeball with the enemy. I had never really looked at a fly before.

The fly stopped pacing. I wondered if it wanted to bite me. No, it was probably too busy wondering if I were going to kill it.

Bothersome fly! Why in the world would anyone create a fly in the first place? What was God thinking?

'Well, fly, don't just stand there!"

The fly replied by dancing on the mole.

"Say something!"

The fly looked earnestly into my eyes.

"Well?"

I concentrated as hard as I could. I felt my anger loosening. I placed my eye about two inches from the fly's black body. I was much closer to it than I had been to the deer mouse. I wondered: do flies really bite? My mother said they do, but no fly ever bit me.

"You don't want to bite me, do you, fly?"

As if to reassure me, the fly gaily flew away, circling around my shoulders with great style, and returned to the mole on my arm.

Soon I noticed two feeler-like things waving about like little arms. It looked as if the fly were using those feelers the way cats use paws to clean themselves. One by one I began questioning all the things I had ever been taught about flies.

Flies bite. Really? I wasn't so sure.

Flies are a lesser life form. Not true. This fly chose to land on the same mole again and again. Apparently it had a memory.

Flies are dirty. I didn't see any dirt.

Flies are pests, a punishment sent by God. That made no sense at all. The fly on my arm actually looked as though it wanted to communicate with me. The longer I stared at it, the more I became convinced its life was as important to it as mine was to me.

And then I realized what was happening: the fly was my first teacher of the day. My face burned with shame. I had almost killed the fly the way I had killed the spider the other night. Brave, brave little fly! Will you forgive me?

The fly took off and did figure eights around my head. I knew it would be back.

When it landed on my arm again, I looked at the fly with new eyes to see how it might teach me. I made my breathing imperceptible as I quieted myself enough to listen. I put my face as close to the fly as I dared. For a moment, I forgot my sore knee.

I remembered Aron's advice and wordlessly tried to get behind the fly's eyes. I concentrated only on making a connection with that tiny, significant creature.

"A-a-at last I have your a-a-a-attention."

The fly startled me! It spoke from the same place Aron did, from inside me.

After those six words, I saw it wipe its brow with its left feeler.

"S-s-sometimes you are not mindful enough of your s-s-s-size," the fly complained. "You know, if I couldn't s-s-see all around me, you might have k-k-k-killed me!"

"I'm sorry," I murmured.

"You th-th-think you know it all. You th-th-think you're better than us a-a-ants, moths, butterflies, s-s-spiders -- all of us bugs!"

I blushed with embarrassment. What the fly was saying was true.

"I said I was sorry. How can I make amends? I do want to get on with my learning. Are you my teacher?" I asked earnestly.

The fly buzzed off, circled around an old cedar, came back and landed, then took off again, as if it couldn't decide to stay or go. It returned and landed on the same mole on my arm, and said:

"Y-y-y-you want everything d-d-d-done your way! A-a-all you can th-th-think about is what y-y-you need. I c-c-can't teach you a-a-anything!"

I didn't know flies could be so angry. The angrier the fly got, the more it stuttered.

"Of course I'm s-s-s-stuttering," the fly said with rising annoyance. "You'd be s-s-s-stuttering, too, if s-s-someone the s-s-size of that cedar began s-s-s-swatting at you!"

"Please now dear fly...." I pleaded.

"And d-d-d-don't you patronize me with th-th-that 'dear fly' stuff," it added huffily.

"And don't you be so touchy." Now I was annoyed. "I said I was sorry. Won't you please accept my apologies and teach me my lesson?"

"The t-t-trouble with y-y-y-you is that y-y-y-you see only straight ahead," the fly grumbled. "Y-y-y-you move too fast, y-y-y-you don't look from s-side to s-s-side, and y-y-y-you never l-l-l-look behind you, now d-d-d-do you?"

"I like to see where I'm going instead of where I've been," I said with increasing impatience. "I can always turn around if I want to see behind me. In fact, I can turn any which way I choose."

"There you g-g-g-go ag-g-g-gain, s-s-speaking like a know-it-all," the fly retorted angrily "If you c-c-could see better, if y-y-y-you had eyes like mine, you wouldn't have f-f-f-fallen."

The fly flew off into the woods. My whole body twisted and turned in my effort to keep the fly in sight. Then it landed back on my arm.

"You s-s-see?" it practically shouted.

I wasn't sure I did.

"Wake up! Y-y-y-you are not watching c-c-closely enough. Honestly, you kn-kn-kn-know-it-alls are the hardest p-p-p-people in the Universe to t-t-t-teach."

I brought my right eye -- my better seeing eye -- right up to the fly. My eye was open so wide it watered. If I had moved any closer, I would have batted the fly with my eyelashes.

"Th-th-that's close enough," said the fly firmly. "The f-f-f-first thing you must kn-kn-know is that f-f-f-flies don't get c-c-caught in s-s-spider webs. W-w-w-we fly there at the e-e-end of our l-l-l-life cycle so s-s-spiders have some food and we k-k-keep the earth cl-cl-clean. You m-m-must have n-n-n-noticed n-n-n-nothing in n-n-nature is wasted. So for g-g-g-goodness sake, s-s-stop killing the s-s-s-spiders and s-s-stop breaking their w-w-webs with your blasted stick. Y-y-y-you are interrupting the f-f-flow of life."

I pondered its last remark. I thought I finally was beginning to understand what the fly wanted me to understand. The fly had eyes that could turn around in its eye sockets. It could see in all directions.

My eyes couldn't do what the fly's eyes could. The fly was right. I only saw straight ahead and a little from side to side and up and down. Unless, of course, I moved my head.

The fly rubbed its tiny feelers together as if it were applauding. I must have gotten the right answer.

The fly jumped and pirouetted around like a circus clown. I was certain I had gotten the right answer.

Suddenly, I saw myself as I had been earlier that morning, charging up and down the path, going from the dock to the back rock to the cottage to the dock. I was only looking forward -- not side to side or up and down or even back. Just forward! On the back rock, I walked right past the ants. I had actually been scornful of them.

The fly's eyes got larger and larger. They were now so big I felt they must be at least as big as mine. Now we were looking at each other as equals. I watched in awe as the fly showed me how versatile its eyes were, swirling and turning this way and that.

Then I understood. The fly's eyes helped me to see myself.

Earlier, when I barged through the woods, I had my mind made up about the way my teaching was going to take place. I was too rigid to see new ways of learning. I literally had to fall to stop myself so I could look and listen with clearer eyes, clearer ears.

I blinked my eyes to loosen the intensity of my concentration. I looked at my arm. The fly was gone. I looked around. I saw a lot of flies buzzing in the air, but I couldn't tell which fly was my teacher.

The woods were brimming with life. I knew each tree had its own separate pulse, but I never felt it so strongly before. I heard and saw so much I worried my ears and eyes would fill up and explode.

I shifted my consciousness back outside myself when I heard some kind of small critter tiptoeing down the path. Its footsteps were loud and precise to my new ears. I guessed it was one of the cats. When it came into view, I saw I was right. It was Twyla. She can see and feel everything, too.

I scratched Twyla under her chin as she rubbed her body against my face. I love her purr. I sensed she was telling me it was okay to stand up now.

I stood. She was right. My knee felt fine.

I tried walking. No pain.

I followed Twyla back toward the cottage, slowly, cautiously, listening, looking, wishing I, too, had a tail to hold straight in the air.

"Hey there! Anybody home?"

I recognized the voice. Cassie came running down the path to get me.

The noise that came with the voice scattered my thoughts of flies and learning all over the woods.

"Hey, lassie! Are ye here?"

It was Mrs. McCrae, the woman who lived at the landing where we parked our car. She was the other person who was supposed to check up on me. Her house had one of the few telephones on the lake. She was a school teacher long before I was born, and my parents trusted her as much as they trusted Doc.

"I'm here! I'm coming!" I called back. I had a sinking feeling in the pit of my stomach that something dire had happened to Granny Rose. You know what they say, bad news travels fast and no news is good news.

"My, my," said Mrs. McCrae, "the older I get, the longer these paths become. Where are ye, wee one?'

Mrs. McCrae's bulky frame slowly came into view. She has the smallest ankles of anyone I have ever seen, and one of the biggest smiles. Her arms were full of fresh vegetables from her garden. She always grows more food than she and her husband can eat.

"Here ye are, lassie! Now before ye get to worrying, I want ye to know yer Granny Rose is doing fine."

Mrs. McCrae is the only person I know who calls me lassie. My mother calls her "the salt of the earth." She is almost as old as my Granny Rose and occasionally she takes me fishing with her. My father is always envious of our fishing expeditions because she is known to be the best fisher person on the lake. She knows where the big ones are.

"Ah, now, will ye look at yerself!"

I always liked listening to her lilting Canadian/ Scottish accent.

"Ye're all dusty -- covered with pine needles the way ye are! Here now, I brought ye some corn and some wee melons."

"Thank you, Mrs. McCrae," I said. "You didn't need to come all the way over here to give me these."

"Well actually, I didn't," she said. "I came over to give ye a message from yer ma. She called to say they wouldn't be arriving back at the lake until week's end. She's worried about ye, lass. She wanted me to come out here and see how ye might be faring. She didn't expect to leave ye alone so long."

"But I'm loving this time alone!" I exclaimed.

"If ye say so," Mrs. McCrae said, not totally convinced. "Ye look all right and ye haven't burned the cottage down yet."

"I'm fine. Truly," I said.

"I have a feeling I interrupted something, lassie. Ye look a little dazed."

"Sort of," I said. "I was sitting on the path talking to a fly."

"Were ye, now?" Mrs. McCrae asked in a puzzled voice.

On cue, a fly landed again on my arm. I touched it lovingly with my finger. I looked at Mrs. McCrae, wanting to watch her watch me with my new friend.

No such luck. Mrs. McCrae's attention was on Cassie. She was busy scratching Cassie behind the ears.

The fly zipped off out of sight, back toward the outhouse. I was beginning to resent Mrs. McCrae's presence. I wanted to sit on a rock in the sun and think about the fly, my eyes, my rigid way of seeing the world. I wanted to sit under a tree and work on my tapestry and let my thoughts go where they would. I wanted to be quiet. I wanted to pull out the yellow yarn.

"I guess I do things a little differently when I'm here alone," I mumbled, not knowing what else to say.

Mrs. McCrae's smile widened. Her concentration was back on me. She took me by the hand and together we walked back toward the cottage. My hand felt very small in hers. When she squeezed it, I had a fleeting sense of how small the fly must have felt when I was swatting at it. I didn't like feeling small.

"I was thinking some fresh fish might taste mighty good, lassie," Mrs. McCrae said. "Let us catch some bass for dinner, aye? I've brought a whole bucket of frogs with me."

My stomach tightened. Not frogs. Not for bait! Frogs are my teachers. How in the world was I going to explain that to an ardent fisher person?

"I don't feel like fishing today, Mrs. McCrae. I'll tell you what, though. I'll paddle you to your favorite cove."

"Anything ye say, lassie. My fingers are itching to get my fishing line in the water. We'd better go right away before the sun gets too high."

I wondered if Aron knew Mrs. McCrae would be bringing frogs for bait.

After a quick lunch of pickles and cheese on crackers (I'm not a very good cook!), Mrs. McCrae and I went out on the lake in the canoe for our "stringer full." I paddled as I said I would, keeping the canoe hovering near shore and avoiding rocks and water-soaked logs. Mrs. McCrae sat in the bow of the canoe with her back toward me.

I heard the frogs jumping around in the frog bucket. I was so busy listening to the jumping and the splashing that I stopped hearing other sounds. I even stopped feeling Mrs. McCrae's presence, which was a pretty amazing feat by itself.

We entered Mrs. McCrae's favorite cove, and I put my paddle down. The canoe began to drift wherever the breeze took it.

Mrs. McCrae dropped her trolling line in the lake and rigged up her fly rod. She was so busy thinking about catching the big one that I knew she didn't want to talk any more than I did. I was relieved not to worry about making idle chit-chat. I wanted to concentrate on the frogs.

There was one problem. I knew that soon Mrs. McCrae was going to ask me to pass her the frog bucket. After all, she brought the frogs for bait. What was I going to say to her?

"Hand me the frog bucket, will ye, lassie?"

Oh, no, I thought. Mrs. McCrae reached behind her with her left hand.

"Okay, but in a minute," I said. "How about casting with a jitterbug for a little bit while I look at the frogs you brought?" I pleaded.

"No problem, lassie," said Mrs. McCrae, as she reached down in front of her for her tackle box. She opened it while I opened the lid of the bait bucket. I reached in my hand and picked out a very small grass frog, probably the smallest one she had caught.

"Hi, sweet thing," I said softly.

The small frog pulled hard to free itself.

"I'm not going to hurt you, little one," I continued softly. "I'm going to let you go. I'm going to find a way to let all of you go. Tell your friends not to worry."

I had to speak softly so Mrs. McCrae wouldn't know what I was planning. Unfortunately, my soft words were of no comfort to the frog. It yanked and pulled. It tried everything it knew to free itself from my grasp.

"Stop pulling and twisting so hard, little frog," I said softly. "I want to learn from you. Sit! Sit quietly so we can talk."

All at once I realized I was doing what Twyla had done with the mouse. I was manipulating the frog. I was so shocked I let the frog go. The small frog jumped into the lake and swam away.

Drat, I said to myself. One teacher gone.

No problem.

I leaned over and picked another frog out of the bucket.

"Hello, pretty," I cooed. Cooing is my way of talking when I want to be liked.

This frog, too, pulled to free itself. This one looked like the one I saw on the green, watching the turtles dance.

"Don't be afraid," I said. "I won't hurt you. If you sit quietly, I'll let you go. I hope you have something to teach me."

The small frog sat quietly, and true to my word, I let it go. It, too, jumped into the lake and swam away.

Another teacher gone.

Then it occurred to me I was acting the same way I had with the fly that morning. I was not listening. I was still trying to do everything my way. The frogs probably thought I was a know-it-all, too.

I bent down and picked up a third frog.

"Hello, frog."

I stopped talking baby talk. I talked to the frog the way I talk to a person I respect.

Mrs. McCrae whistled in the front of the canoe. Her whistle always said she loved to fish more than anything else in the world. She whistled the loudest of all when she got a strike. I kept my fingers crossed hoping she'd get a bite, because if Mrs. McCrae caught a fish with the jitterbug, she might not care about using the frogs as bait.

"I'm here to let you go," I whispered to the frog. "Please, could we talk first? I won't hurt you. I promise."

I gently stroked the young frog's back. I wanted to soothe it, but all I could see was how afraid of me -- how desperate -- it was.

I stopped stroking and stopped speaking. I tried to do what I tried with the fly -- see the world through the frog's eyes.

I prepared to be a frog by sitting like one, in a deep squat, quite an accomplishment in a canoe. I pretended Mrs. McCrae was a huge giant who could either kill me or, if she didn't use me as bait, set me free. I tried yanking and pushing and straining the way the frog did when I held it. The canoe rocked precariously from side to side.

"Hey!" Mrs. McCrae yelled. "What are ye doing back there, lassie? Stop rocking the canoe, or we'll all go into the drink just as sure as the sun will go down. What are ye doing?"

"Nothing," I said innocently. "I'm just talking to the frogs."

"Ye're certainly in a strange mood today," Mrs. McCrae mused.

I let go of the frog I was holding, but instead of jumping into the lake as the others did, this one jumped down to the bottom of the canoe. The frog was watching me as closely as I had been watching it a few moments before. I leaned down in the bottom of the canoe to be as close to the frog as I could.

"Lassie, ye're scaring the fish with all that wiggling around," Mrs. McCrae complained. "Sit still, aye?"

Mrs. McCrae turned around this time and looked at me sitting on the floor of the canoe. She looked just as worried as the frog.

"I'm okay. I just wanted to get closer to the frog. Hey! I think you have a nibble there!"

Mrs. McCrae's pole suddenly arched over toward the lake. A strike! Her attention zipped back to her line and a whistle burst forth from between her lips. Immediately I went back to being a frog.

Small frog and big I continued looking at one another. I wondered if it was too afraid to move, as Twyla's mouse had been. Or was it indeed a teacher, waiting for school to start?

The warmth of the sun was helpful. As it melted into my skin, I got more and more relaxed. I began to feel and think what I thought were obvious frog thoughts:

I like the sun.

I'm afraid.

Please set me free.

Please free my friends.

I want my mama.

I want a lily pad.

Let me alone.

Let me drink up the sun.

"Which leg is the tired leg?" asked the frog unexpectedly as it hopped onto my knee.

I jumped at the sound of the frog's voice, high and squeaky. I was surprised that the frog trusted me enough to come so close, surprised to hear such a good question. Instead of pushing me out of my thoughts, it pulled me deeper in.

"What do you mean?" I asked, feeling confused.

"Just what I said," the frog squeaked again. "You know the leg you were holding me by. Was it working harder or was the free leg working harder?"

I thought for a moment, envisioning the small frog kicking mightily to free itself.

"The free leg," I answered quietly, "the one doing all the kicking."

"Wrong," said the frog in a suddenly low, authoritative voice.

"But your free leg was the one kicking and swinging to free you from my grasp," I said.

"Pick me up again," said the frog, returning to its squeaky voice. "Watch me a second time. You're not awake yet. You're still distracted by outer noises."

The frog pushed itself into my hand. I tightened my grasp on one of its legs, and once again it pulled and strained to get away, kicking its free leg vigorously.

"I hope you're watching," shouted the frog, "because this takes a lot of energy."

The frog's voice got higher and squeakier as it began to tire.

"I am! I am!" I answered, trying very hard not to be a know-it-all. It still seemed to me the free leg thrusting and pushing was doing all the work. The frog interrupted my thoughts.

"You do have trouble looking and seeing at the same time, don't you? Pretend you're a frog being held by a great big person. Be me!"

I tried to do as the frog suggested. Again, I sank into that drowsy space, so deep that I barely noticed Mrs. McCrae reaching for a net to land her fish and casting her line back out.

I moved so deeply inside myself, I slipped right behind the eyes of the frog.

It didn't take long before I understood what the frog meant. The kicking leg was free. It wasn't the harder-working leg at all. The leg I was holding was the one that was pulling mightily to no avail, the one that was bound and tired, filled with fear, aching from overextension.

"What conclusions do you come to?" asked the frog. Its voice, although still high, sounded hollow. I didn't smell fear any more.

I said, "If I move like your free leg and try different things, I won't be nearly as tired as I will be if I stay tight, closed, and controlled by what frightens me -- spiders and ghost maidens."

"Very good, very good!" bellowed the frog. "At last I have your attention. Now then, give me some examples of what you want to learn from me."

"I was hoping to learn to like myself more," I said, "so I could feel the way I felt when I danced with the turtles. I want to learn the words to the turtle song. I want to know how to keep my moonstone safe. As you have probably guessed, I don't like myself much when I kill spiders. I've been told I need to open my heart so I can love and trust all I am and all that is around me. That's the whole truth."

My words rushed out.

"Very good, very good again." The frog's voice stayed low and round. "Be free. Don't tighten. Let go. Trust all that is!"

"What is all that is?" I asked.

"God, to you," the frog answered.

"Maybe I need to shake myself like you shook your free leg."

Mrs. McCrae's voice cut into my thoughts.

"Lassie, lassie, we won't have very many fish for yer and my dinner tonight if ye keep on shaking and swaying this way."

I looked at the frog again. I realized I held myself tightly each time I judged one of my friends. I was always tight when I didn't feel good about myself. Next time I feel that way, I thought, I'll try moving a muscle, or shouting for joy, or singing. Next time, I'll shake!

The small frog jumped up onto the seat behind me. I knew what it needed to do: it was time for the frog to go. I twisted around and stroked it gently one last time and said "Be free! Don't tighten! Let go! Trust all that is, friend frog! Swim away."

Mrs. McCrae's irritated voice pulled me out of myself again.

"Ye're not letting another frog go, are ye, lassie?"

"Oh, you wouldn't have liked that one," I answered. "It was big and hairy and had lots of teeth. Yuk."

Mrs. McCrae laughed, indulging me just a little longer. I knew I was running out of time.

I hummed thanks as my new friend swam away. The tune I hummed was the one the turtles danced to, the one whose words I still didn't know.

Instead of diving to the bottom of the lake, the frog I just released began to dance from one lily pad to the next. I was certain it liked my singing.

So I hummed the tune over and over. Mrs. McCrae began singing along with me. She had a clear tenor voice, high for a man and low for a woman. Her pitch was as true as a cardinal's song. At first I sang louder than she, and then she sang louder than I. The remaining frogs hopped and bounced about in the bucket.

Without missing a beat, I picked up the bucket and opened the lid as our song rose into the trees by the lake. I tipped the bucket over and dumped all the remaining frogs into the lake.

Now a dozen frogs circled and danced from one lily pad to another. A dragonfly appeared and vibrated its wings in celebration.

"Be free, frogs! Be free, don't tighten, let go, trust all that is!" I said as the dragonfly guided the frogs to shore.

"Hey there, lassie," shouted Mrs. McCrae in a tone that was decidedly not playful. "What have ye done now? It took me a full hour to catch those frogs this morning."

"I know, I know," I replied. "I guess I got caught up in the song. I got feeling so happy I wanted the frogs to be happy, too."

"First ye rock the boat, then ye sing and scare away the fish, and now ye go dumping all my wee frogs into the lake," Mrs. McCrae complained.

"But they're not your frogs," I insisted.

"Lassie, say what ye will. Ye've never done this with my frogs before. Yer pa will never believe what ye've done, if I choose to tell him."

"Let's not fish any more, Mrs. McCrae," I said. "I think I'd better go home. Doc'll be wondering where I am."

Mrs. McCrae looked inquiringly at me over her shoulder. It was obvious from her expression she was a little worried about me. I knew I had to say something quickly to make her laugh, or she might make me go with her to her house, concluding I wasn't old enough to stay by myself in our cottage. Mrs. McCrae slowly brought in her line.

"Next time we go fishing," I said jokingly, "I'll bring along a deck of cards and we'll play Go Fish!"

"Right," she said, her tone softening, "so ye can throw the cards in the lake as well as the frogs!"

Mrs. McCrae was returning to her cheerful self. I was well aware fishing was serious business for her. It was no small thing when I threw her frogs into the lake.

I watched Mrs. McCrae's back intently. Then I heard a deep sigh. She carefully put down her pole and pulled in the two fish she caught that were on the stringer, hanging over the side of the canoe. She was ready for me to start paddling.

"Oh well, we've still got a good dinner hanging here," she said, nodding her head towards the stringer. "One bonnie wee fish for you, lassie, and one for me.

My husband Percy will have to think of something else to eat. They're not the biggest fish in the world, but they'll do."

I didn't answer. The thought of eating the fish made me feel sick. I tried not to look at the two lone fish.

"Mrs. McCrae?" I asked tentatively.

"No, ye don't! I know what ye're thinking. Don't ask me."

"Please?"

"But it's food, lassie."

"Please? Do the fish a favor," I persisted.

"I canna believe ye're asking me to do this," Mrs. McCrae lamented.

"Yes," I said quietly, shaking my head up and down.

Mrs. McCrae slowly turned around to face me. "Understand, ye're the only person in this world I would do this fer. Ye know that, aye?"

She grabbed the stringer and freed the fish, one at a time.

"Now are ye happy, lassie?" she grumbled.

"Happier than you can imagine," I said gratefully. "Relieved, too."

"Ye're wanting to let those fish go boggles my brain," Mrs. McCrae said, shaking her head in dismay. "Methinks I'll have to find meself a new fishing buddy."

"I'm sorry about that," I said contritely.

"So am I," Mrs. McCrae said soberly, determined to change the subject. "Let's be heading back to yer cottage so I can take a look around and see how ye're really doing. Yer ma wants a report. She thinks ye should come down and stay with me."

"No, really, I'm fine by myself," I responded quickly. "I'm in the midst of a bunch of projects. I couldn't bear to leave any of them even for a little while."

All the way home, while I worked at convincing Mrs. McCrae to let me stay by myself, I heard the same little tune over and over again. I kept apologizing about the frogs, but I also felt enormously happy.

"Won't you stay and have dinner with me?" I urged. "It doesn't have to be pickles and cheese. I make really good corn."

"The good Lord makes really good corn," Mrs. McCrae quickly interjected.

"Please stay and eat your wonderful corn with me."

"I think not, lassie. I've got some fishing to do before I go home, before I call yer parents."

"You'll tell them I'm fine, won't you?" I asked anxiously.

"Yes, I'll tell them ye're fine."

I let out a deep sigh.

"I'm the one who's not fine," groused Mrs. McCrae as she turned around, looked at me in the eye, and winked.

CHAPTER FIVE

I spent the evening and the next day quietly. The weather turned cold and rainy, so I stayed in the cottage close to the fire, working hard on my tapestry. I wanted to surprise my mother with a finished product. She thinks I never finish anything.

I had plenty of lessons from the fly and the frog to ponder. Their teachings were like homework assignments. Thinking about how to listen wasn't enough. I had to remember to listen with my heart.

I hooked in three triangles. Or were they trees? It was fun watching the tapestry create itself. When evening came, I made lines and squares, like a sidewalk or a chess game.

As I hooked along, I thought about Mrs. McCrae. What did I learn from her? She was alive. She was a real teacher. I didn't listen to her nearly as hard as I did the frog and the fly. Next time I must, I thought.

My hand went up to my pouch. I touched it longingly at least ten times a day. Maybe the moonstone wasn't so magical after all. Maybe it belonged to Aron?

The fire was unusually noisy that night. It popped and crackled as I clicked and snapped my hook-latching tool. Was the fire a teacher, too? Was it alive?

It felt as if the fire were thinking. The more it thought, the smokier the room became. I decided smoke was like a thought, like a new idea struggling to be born.

I alternated between keeping my eyes on the tapestry and on the fire. Both kept changing. I wondered what the fire was trying to say. I wondered what the tapestry was trying to become. If I could listen better, I knew I'd know.

I put my tool down and concentrated on the fire. I tried to get behind the eyes of the fire the way I got behind the eyes of the fly and the frog. But the fire had no eyes I could see. There were at least as many colors in the fire as I had in my yarn bag.

Pop! Pop! Pop!

The fire popped like the tap, tap, tap of a conductor's baton. Clearly, the fire was trying to get my attention.

Pop! It was louder this time.

Three pops.

Three cracks.

Pop!

Pop crack, pop crack, pop crack, pop!

It repeated itself. I began to feel the rhythm.

Pop crack, pop crack, pop crack, pop! It felt like the beat of the dance of the turtles. I couldn't get that turtle tune out of my mind. I hummed it all the time.

Pop crack, pop crack, pop crack, pop!

If D-flat is the universal key for songs of all living things -- my music teacher told my class that -- maybe pop crack, pop crack, pop crack, pop is the universal rhythm.

Step slide, step slide, step slide, clap!

I began to tap out the dance.

Wag my tail and turn around!

The steps were still in my body.

The rhythm was the same. I was sure of it.

I stood up and went step sliding and clapping around the room.

My body remembered all the subtle variations. I didn't think about what to do. I began the dance around the log table in the middle of the room.

Pop crack, pop crack, pop crack, pop!

I danced past the fireplace, the stove, the desk, and whirled once more past the fireplace. Around and around I went. The feeling of freedom was coming back -- at least a little of it.

Perhaps, if I kept doing it, I'd fly again.

Pop crack, pop crack, pop crack, pop! Step slide, step slide, step slide, clap! Bless the earth, bless the sky, turn around, pounce!

The cottage creaked and swayed as if it were trying to lift itself off of its cinder block foundation.

I stopped dancing. Incredibly, the cottage slowly began to move. The cottage, the furniture, the dishes, the pots and pans all rattled and shook.

I hurried to the fire to see if a log had fallen, causing the sparks I saw in the air around me.

The fire was unchanged, faithfully keeping the beat.

Pop crack, pop crack, pop crack, pop!

Pop! Crack! Snap! Pop!

Circling and dancing made me dizzy. I sank into a chair. My world turned around and around, faster and faster. The cottage spun wildly.

I looked out the window. I couldn't tell if the little sparks of light I saw outside were from fireflies or the lighthouse on the other side of the lake as it whizzed past my view. Or, was it the moon blinking?

Popcracksnappop!

The cottage sighed, groaned and came to a stop. The fire began to purr.

Slowly I got to my feet. I was still very dizzy.

Everything was unusually quiet.

I walked unsteadily to the center of the room and silently looked around. Cassie was pacing uneasily and the cats were rubbing against my ankles. When Cassie went back under the bed, Twyla and Lizzie asked to be let out.

What had happened? The cottage seemed all right, nothing was broken, the fire was undisturbed. I was all right, and so were Cassie, Lizzie and Twyla.

I opened the door and let the cats out. They hurried between my legs and disappeared into the darkness. I looked around. All I could see were lots of little lights.

As my eyes got used to the dark, I thought I saw something familiar. Was it my circle of turtles?

Yes! It had to be. The little lights were lanterns, lighting the green outside each little turtle's shell.

Impulsively, I looked up and inspected the rafters of the cottage. It wasn't a cottage at all. I was standing in the middle of a great big turtle shell.

Somehow or other, I had danced myself back to the turtles' green. Or, maybe I danced myself forward into a different turtles' green. I didn't know. I was getting more comfortable about not knowing the answers to my questions.

Lanterns swung from poles directly outside my turtle shell. The shells of the turtles ringed a beautiful pool, glistening in the lantern light. One white water lily rested in the middle of the pool, closed up tightly the way all water lilies do at night or on a cloudy day. Everyone knows water lilies need sunlight to open.

I stepped out of my turtle shell so I could see better. The turtles were there, stretching and swinging, preparing to dance. Twyla came out of the darkness and hovered close around my ankles.

Much to my surprise, Aron was sitting next to my turtle shell. Both cats ran to him and purred contentedly. He was dressed in full Indian regalia, with his white hair hanging loosely around his shoulders. He was smoking a peace pipe. I could smell the sage as the smoke reached my nose.

"Hi, Aron! It's me! I'm back!"

Aron smiled, patted the ground beside him, and said, "Come sit down!"

I did as he said, and together we silently watched all the activity going on around us. Everyone was busy, but at first I could only see a very small portion of what was happening. As my ears and eyes became more adjusted to the darkness, I saw and heard more.

Some turtles were dressed in costume, and others were changing into them. Some were dressing like people, but some were dressing like animals and plants and minerals. I saw one turtle dressed like poison ivy and another like a red-tailed hawk.

Only Aron was dressed like an Indian. He did not seem to be in costume, though, any more than I was. Everyone else seemed to be preparing for Halloween night or a masquerade ball.

"This," Aron said, "is a very special night. Everyone except me is dressing as the animal, plant or mineral they most fear. But I have another job to do. You are invited to join us if you would like."

I looked down at my baggy pants, sweatshirt and bare feet.

"But I have no costume -- only what I have on."

"Do not worry," answered Aron, articulating each syllable as he spoke. "You can be anyone or anything you want. Ordinarily, you would dress as the person you are or the person you most want to be."

Twyla hissed and pushed Lizzie with her paw so Aron would stroke only her.

"Tonight is diffcrent," Aron continued. "Tonight we invite you to change into the life-form you most fear. Fear can be a great teacher, too."

That sounded like something Doc might say. In fact, I thought, Aron's voice sounded a little like Doc's.

"The only living thing I'm afraid of is a spider. Yuk! Does that mean I have to go as a spider?" I grimaced.

"That is up to you!"

"But I'm not afraid of anything else," I said.

"Precisely! I do believe you have your answer," Aron replied.

"Hmmm," I groaned as I thought about becoming a spider. "Will changing hurt?" I asked practically.

"Oh, no! It will be fun. You will see. You have done it before!"

True, I thought, I had become a turtle. But I love turtles. I couldn't imagine being a spider.

"Where do I find a spider suit?" I asked.

"You do not. When you are ready to change, you think yourself into any particular spider you want to be. When you can see it, feel it, know it, put your hand to the back of your head and unzip your zipper as you saw me do. It is as simple as that. When you become a spider...."

"Wait a minute! Wait a minute!" I interrupted. "Before I go changing into a spider, you must assure me I'll be able to change back. I don't want to be a spider for the rest of my life. I'll try it for a little while, but then I want to come back to me and my baggy pants and sweatshirt."

"You did not stay a turtle for the rest of your life when your skin turned green, did you?" Aron asked. "You thought yourself into a turtle, granted unknowingly, and you thought yourself back. You change into a spider and back the same way. When you return, you will look the same as you do now. But inside you will be changed. I guarantee it."

"How changed?"

Aron smiled one of his most beguiling smiles. He patted my knee as if to say "Relax, I have told you all you need to know. When you need to know more, you will."

Out loud he said: "Do not tighten. Let go. Trust all that is. Try to remember what you have learned and remain open to greater insight that can only come your way by being a spider."

I scratched my head despairingly. My lack of trust was showing, and it embarrassed me. I thought about running back into the cottage. But the cottage was now a turtle shell. If only I had the moonstone. . .if only . . . .

That was all I needed to think. Suddenly, there it was in my lap! My moonstone! I grabbed it quickly and put it into the pouch hanging around my neck. "Hey, Aron, it came back! My moonstone came back. Did you make that happen? If you did, thank you, thank you, thank you."

Aron smiled, but said nothing.

I tasted the smell of sage. I welcomed the distraction. The sage smelled wise and tasted old. Let go. Trust all that is. Surely Aron's right. If I needed to know more, I would.

Aron interrupted my thoughts. "You see, tonight we celebrate the star goddess, the caretaker of the earth and all life. Tonight the star goddess is with us as a water lily. As the water lily opens, so do we. When her petals unfold, we celebrate our own unfolding, our own learning. As her heart opens, so do our hearts."

I looked at the water lily, the glistening white bud in the center of the dark blue pool.

"Wait," I interjected, "water lilies open only in daylight. Everyone knows that."

"Watch," Aron replied with a smile.

"I will be leaving soon," Aron went on. "I must start my long journey, now that everyone is almost ready to begin the dance. If you want to join the others, you had better hurry."

I quickly closed my eyes to think about the kind of spider I wanted to be. I had difficulty envisioning one because all spiders look alike to me -- except for the big, furry water spiders that live under our dock. Other than those, I had never noticed differences among spiders.

While I considered my options, I suddenly realized I felt as if I could do anything, now I had my moonstone back. I could be the person I had always struggled to be. It didn't matter how the moonstone came to me or why. The only thing important was that I had it. It was mine, safely tucked into my pouch. The moonstone made me feel as strong as I needed to be.

"One last thing . . . ." Aron broke into my reverie. I opened my eyes as he spoke. "If you desire to change. . . ."

"I do! I do!" I exclaimed. "You know I want to be a better person, a better daughter.."

"Well then," said Aron, "listen carefully. You are to place a treasure, something you value, at the edge of the pool, as your way of giving thanks to the star goddess for the energy that will help you become who or what you most want to become. A treasure in this context is a gift that comes from the heart. By giving the star goddess what you love best, you give all. By giving all, you demonstrate your commitment to change."

I winced when I thought about giving a gift I loved. I had only one thing to give. I touched my pouch.

"All I have to give is my moonstone," I said mournfully.

"Then give her that," Aron replied simply.

Reluctantly, I pulled out the pouch from under my sweatshirt and loosened the draw string. I took out the moonstone, warm now from being close to my heart. I loved this moonstone much too much to want to give it away. Would the star goddess like another pretty stone or a bunch of flowers perhaps?

"But you do not love another stone or the flowers nearly as much as you love the moonstone," Aron said. He was right.

With great sadness, I tucked the moonstone back into the pouch and walked slowly down towards the pool. Giving the moonstone to the star goddess was not going to be easy, but I had to do it if I wanted to change -- and I did want to change.

On the way, I saw one of my frog friends from Mrs. McCrae's bait bucket sitting on one of the lily pads in the pool. It was busy thinking itself into the form of a woman, most certainly a particular woman. The lily pad was having trouble supporting the weight of this change, so the frog was stuck somewhere in between its frog self and the woman it wanted to become.

"Can I help?" I asked.

"Oh, you again! No, thank you!" squeaked the frog. "Only I can change myself."

"I agree," I nodded. "But I think you'll find it's easier to become a person if you get off the lily pad."

The frog looked at me, surprised I could be helpful.

"Yes, indeed! I do believe you're right!" The frog hopped onto the grass around the pool. Its voice was just as squeaky as I remembered it.

The frog concentrated with all its might, and soon I saw gray hair and the familiar small ankles.

"Why do you want to be a woman, this particular woman?" I asked.

"Because this woman wanted to use me as bait," the frog retorted. My frog friend was trying to become Mrs. McCrae.

"Tonight I shall do my best to learn about understanding my fear of that blasted woman who caught me. Then, perhaps I'll never get caught for bait again. Yip-pee!"

The frog's transformation was almost complete. Mrs. McCrae's smile was suddenly before me.

"What are ye going to be?" she asked.

"I'm going to be a spider," I said.

"Afraid of a wee thing like a spider?" asked Mrs. McCrae with her Scottish/Canadian accent.

"Yep!" I answered. "I have no idea why. A spider never did anything to me."

"Well, lassie, ye'll be sure to learn tonight."

Mrs. McCrae left me so she could stamp around in the grass and look for frogs. Even now her frame looked too large to be supported by her small ankles. As with my other night visitors, her costume had an imaginary zipper at the back of the neck.

Once I got to the pool, I slowly reached into my pouch and pulled out my beloved moonstone. I put it down carefully at the edge of the pool, and looked at it with enormous appreciation and sadness. My gift looked so pretty sitting there. I had to say, the moonstone fit perfectly in this environment. The star goddess will take good care of it, I thought, so I'll just have to say goodbye to my precious stone.

I sat down and looked at my reflection in the pool to see if I had begun to change. No. I was still me. I hadn't become a spider yet. Why not?

"Hurry," shouted Aron. "Change, or you will miss the fun."

Ha! I thought, they think this is fun? I was finally reunited with my moonstone, and now look.

I glanced up and saw Mrs. McCrae circling around in the grass. She was having a great time. I thought if the frog had the courage to be Mrs. McCrae and look that happy, then maybe being a spider could be fun after all.

I closed my eyes a second time. I still hadn't thought of a particular spider I might consider being. I thought of the spider inside my nightgown when I put it on the other night. That was a dreadful moment. I thought about the spider that dropped down the inside of my collar from the ceiling of the outhouse. That was worse.

I couldn't bear thinking about those spiders, much less becoming one of them.

Then it came to me: I'll be Charlotte, the wise brown spider in *Charlotte's Web*, a book I had read a long time ago. I always liked her.

I thought hard about Charlotte, reviewing all I could remember about her. She was small as spiders go, brown, fragile but strong. That's what I wanted to be, fragile but strong. I reached my hand to the back of my head. . . I felt around. Charlotte was very good-natured... yes, more than anything, she was very good-natured....

Presto! I was engulfed in a shower of brown and yellow light. I felt my center of gravity drop, and I became spectacularly lighter as pounds of human flesh and bones disappeared. I placed all my spider arms and legs on the moss to keep my balance.

I heard the voice of Aron. "Let go! Trust all that is!"

I crept over to the edge of the pool for another look. Yikes! I had done it!

I saw myself perched on eight arms and legs. I was Charlotte. I was a spider about the size of a quarter.

I waved at myself with one of my arms. I didn't like the way I looked. To be honest, I hated the way I looked. I did, however, like my eyes.

I could see much more as a spider than I could see as a human. I could see through my reflection in the water as I peered down into the earth beneath the pool. I could see a whole network of paths and alleys made by worms that nourished the earth.

I looked up into the sky. I saw a bird as clearly as if I were holding it in my hands. The stars looked close enough to touch.

I still didn't like the way I felt or looked. I felt creepy and crawly, inside and out.

No one can possibly like me, I thought. But wouldn't God be proud?

I stopped thinking, stopped moving, and started listening to feelings of not being liked enough or not being good enough rumbling about inside me.

Suddenly, I realized I had exposed a secret fear I'd worked my whole life to hide.

No one can like me the way I am, I thought. No one. They can only like me when I get good grades, or make people laugh, or look pretty, or am thin. Well, I was already plenty thin.

These thoughts slashed through me like a dagger, right to the center of my heart.

I'd have to worry about that later. Charlotte wanted to move. I had a world to explore, and dances to dance. Fear is good at waiting. It wasn't going anywhere.

I tried walking on my eight arms and legs. I was reassured to see Aron was nearby in case I got frightened.

I turned and walked back to the green. Turning as a spider was easy, maybe even fun. I did it over and over again. Will I ever get used to being this low to the ground? I wondered. I liked feeling graceful and light.

As I headed back toward Aron, I circled and danced on all my tip-toes and tip-fingers, going up trees, slipping under mushrooms. I climbed into the center of a rose and inhaled its sweet scent. I climbed a birch tree right up to the top, and then I did what I had always imagined doing: I swung down to the ground on a thread of silk -- my own homemade silk. I felt as if I were flying.

Let go. Trust.

Wheeee! This was fun. Aron was right.

I was flying!

I was free!

I no longer felt creepy and crawly. I felt beautiful, and wonderfully complete. I decided I liked being a spider. I was being given a taste of liking who I was. I wanted to hold on to that feeling forever.

I looked up and saw Aron getting ready to go on his journey. I intuitively knew his mission was important. I missed him already.

Oh dear, Aron was having trouble reaching the imaginary zipper of his Indian suit. Without being told, I crawled up Aron's back and touched the magic spot on the back of his neck -- it seemed the natural thing to do.

I shook as Aron's body shuddered. But instead of seeing two turtle claws appear, or two woman's arms covered with green polyester, or two man's arms in a business suit, I saw two huge wings emerge from a sprinkling of black, white and red lights surrounding his body.

One wing, so big and powerful, inadvertently knocked me off Aron's back, and I tumbled into the grass. My arms and legs curled inward, so I fell safely.

I watched Aron become an eagle again -- the most magnificent and blessed creature of the sky. Aron grew and grew.

According to myths, eagles can fly high enough to touch the sun. I was certain Aron was going to do something heroic like that with his powerful wings.

The bigger Aron the eagle became, the smaller I felt. I looked with awe at the eagle feathers that now covered his entire body. Eagle feet replaced the moccasins that had been painted on his Indian suit.

The eagle looked down at me, winked his right eye to thank me for my assistance, and with a surge of power took off like a rocket, going high into the sky.

The air circled and swirled about, flinging me up and dropping me down between blades of grass. Even Mrs. McCrae held onto a weeping willow so she wouldn't be blown over.

Tears of joy tried to come to my spider eyes as I listened to all the watching creatures and plants and minerals, even my moonstone, shout out their blessings to Aron. I didn't cry because spiders have no tears; otherwise, I would have.

"Aron is the carrier of the light for the star goddess, who needs it for her unfolding and ours," one of the smaller turtles explained. "The eagle has to go all the way to the sun to find it."

Even my sharp spider eyes couldn't follow the heavenly messenger that far.

The light from the lanterns was brighter now. I assumed Aron needed the light to find his way back, the way I do when I'm out on the lake at night.

The dancers formed a perfect circle around the pool. Everyone and everything was waiting, barely breathing. We were suspended in time. I remember feeling that way when I wait for the first dip on a roller coaster ride.

"Woof!"

That sound could mean only one thing.

"Woof! Woof!"

Cassie was scratching at the inside of the door of the turtle shell that had replaced the cottage. She wanted to come out. But now? She should have come out with me and the cats before I became a spider.

With surprising ease and a great deal of annoyance, I wriggled my way back to the turtle shell and crawled up the door frame so I could reach the door latch. My spider long legs and arms encircled the latch, and somehow or other I found the strength to lift it. The door swung open, and a dog came bounding out. The dog didn't look like Cassie, my Siberian husky. The dog was an Akita.

Then I understood: Cassie was already in costume.

Cassie was afraid of Suki, the black and white Akita she met regularly in the park in the city. Suki didn't like Cassie at all, and she snarled a lot to demonstrate her displeasure when Cassie was near. Suki was the only dog Cassie feared.

"Cassie/Suki hurry!" I called out. "We're about to begin!"

Cassie/Suki wagged her tail at spider/me on the door latch, and then ran down the stairs and joined the circle.

Deep in the pool, there was a huge rumbling. Everyone was starting to dance because they could no longer stand still.

Oh, dear! They were starting without me! Now what was I to do? I couldn't ask Aron for guidance.

I looked up. Way, way up high, I saw a little flicker of light. The light quickly became as bright as the North Star. The light was solitary -- but clearly alive.

I hung on tightly to the door latch as I tried to decide what to do next. My spider hands and feet were itching and aching to be in the dance.

My eight hands and feet began to move. My whole spider body started to dance on top of the door latch. I slipped swiftly down my silk thread and half-leapt, half-flew over the tips of blades of grass and joined the dancers. My fear of not being accepted was gone.

We circled and danced, circled and danced. I laughed at Mrs. McCrae, singing and dancing with exaggerated gusto. I laughed at Cassie/Suki as she discovered she could bark -- something Siberian huskies can't do but Akitas can; she was dancing and barking at the same time.

Then I heard the tune we were dancing to. It was:

Blueberries swayed on their bushes. The mosquitoes danced, the wild flowers, the fireflies, the chipmunks danced, too. Even the turtle shells moved around and around. Everyone was in the circle, sliding and step-hopping. Lizzie and Twyla were there, dressed like two German shepherd dogs.

The world was alive with music and movement. Only the water lily was closed. Or, had it opened a little? It was hard to tell. The light was brighter now.

I looked up, and all of the other dancers looked up, too.

"Ah! We see it! The great eagle is returning!"

How bold and beautiful Aron the eagle looked as he did swooping figure eights in the sky. He scalloped his way back to Earth, to the water lily and all of us dancing, creating enough joy to feed the spirits of every living being. The light he brought spilled around the circle as far as my eyes could see. It was so bright, I almost forgot it was nighttime.

Although I knew I was dancing, I felt as if I were standing still. My spider eyes felt as large as my spider body. I was all-seeing.

My attention shifted from Aron the eagle to the water lily. It glowed radiantly. I could see all sides of it at once.

Several of its outer white petals had already opened. I knew it was unfolding in the light right before me.

I kept looking at the water lily, wondering when the star goddess would appear. Its petals were still, even though I knew the change was taking place. Change is easiest to comprehend once it is completed.

My spider body felt more and more my own than my human body ever had. I shook my brown center, pretending I had a tail to wag. I was glad I was who – what -- I was.

The water lily opened the rest of its outer white petals. It was the radiant goddess of all life, so regal, so full of love. The light embraced the yellow petals that remained in the center of her bud.

Kya!

The eagle's call took the singing higher, and the turtle song became a round. The harmonies made me feel I would burst with happiness. The formation of dancers changed from one to three circles.

Kya!

Aron the eagle was closer now, so close we stopped dancing.

I held one of my spider hands over my eyes and looked up at Aron the eagle in the blinding white light. I could see the light through my spider arm. I could see it through all of me, inside and out. For a moment, all of the dancers and Aron the eagle were translucent.

I noticed an aura glowing around my hand. It was violet, and pulsed with bursts of rose and yellow. There was power moving through me, coming from both the earth and the sky.

In another moment, I felt the meeting of two energies, the inner and outer, the earth and sky, the dark and the light. I felt a balance outside me, matching a balance inside. I felt my feelings of not being good enough, popular enough, smart enough, slip away.

The water lily had four more yellow petals to open. My spider body shook and vibrated with anticipation.

"Be free!" I heard from somewhere. "Don't tighten! Let go! Trust all that is!"

My heart was singing wildly.

The final burst of color, the final opening was near. There were only three more petals to open. I could feel the presence of the star goddess.

Miraculously, human tears tumbled down my brown spider face. I knew soon I would soar like the eagle, open like the water lily, sing like the world about me. Soon, all would be possible, all would be clear -- even the words to the turtle song.

One more petal opened. The last two petals looked like human hands held in prayer. The light was as bright as the sun.

I was opening, too. I had gone down, I had gone up. There was no other place to go.

My spider skin tightened.

I blessed the earth. I blessed the sky. What more was there?

My breathing became labored.

I had moved. I had stood still. I had sung. I had been silent.

I suddenly realized I was outgrowing my spider body. Was it time to see the star goddess?

"Not yet!" shouted Aron the eagle, as he flew with ease above my head.

Aron the eagle's voice was so powerful it propelled me high into the air.

"First you must practice all you have learned tonight," he shouted.

My spider body dissolved in a burst of sparking blue light. I had my own body back. I couldn't see the water lily. Aron the eagle soared into the sky.

"Come back," I yelled. "The star goddess still has not claimed the moonstone. I see it, down by the pool. I want it back, and I must see the star goddess soak in its light. It is only through the light of the moonstone that the last two petals can open. Will I open my heart in time so I can learn the words to the turtle song? There is so much undone. Please show me the way!"

I shriveled inside myself as I fell back toward the earth. Once again, I curled into a tight ball. Tears blurred my vision, and my body trembled. The trembling changed to little jerks.

I was cold. Disappointment did that. My old fear I was not good enough returned with my human body. I was myself again; I was no longer Charlotte. Even with the light, I was freezing. I kept falling and falling. I landed with a soft thump, next to a familiar sound.

"Purr."

"Lizzie?"

"Purr."

I opened my eyes. I was right. It was Lizzie, my aged Siamese cat, no longer a German shepherd, rubbing and purring against my nose -- my human nose, not my spider nose. Lizzie was cold, too. We were back inside the cottage, which was no longer a turtle shell. My face was wet with tears.

I thought of the star goddess -- if only I could have seen her! I came so close, so close. Lizzie licked my tears with her rough pink tongue.

I looked toward the fireplace. The fire was almost out; no wonder I was cold. I touched my pouch.

The moonstone, of course, was gone. The pouch was empty. Reminding myself of my loss made my heart sink down to my toes, despite my elation at the other events of the night.

I walked shakily over to my tapestry. I picked it up and held it close to the lighted kerosene lamp. Something was different.

There was a new road of many different colors in the tapestry. I couldn't remember doing any of it. Nevertheless, I was enthralled by it.

But my moonstone: would that road in the tapestry lead me to my moonstone? Was it still by the pool? Did the star goddess like my precious gift? Did she know it was from me? Would I ever see it again?

The moonstone glowed in my memory.

Clearly, the time had come to give it back, but I hated doing it. I supposed the star goddess needed it more than I did, so we could all open our hearts. Still, I missed it, and wished it were tucked safely inside my pouch, over my heart. I would have to continue my learning without it.

CHAPTER SIX

It took me well into the next day to remember the details of the night before, when I almost saw the star goddess completely open. I wrote down as many of my thoughts and feelings as I could recall -- I didn't want to forget any of them. There were too many I didn't understand.

I thought about my moonstone most of all. I tried to remember how I felt when I liked who I was, how I felt when I was Charlotte. I wanted to hold on to that particular memory forever.

My parents were expected late in the day or early evening. In some ways it was going to be good to see them, but I assumed their arrival would mean an end to my many adventures. I hoped I was wrong. I was well aware I had a lot more to learn.

I hadn't finished my tapestry -- far from it. I had hoped it would have become something by now. Another project left unfinished.

I hadn't learned to like spiders.

I hadn't learned the words to the turtle song.

I still didn't know how to open my heart, whatever that meant.

And to make everything worse, I had a pile of dishes to do and the cottage to clean before the arrival of my parents.

If only I had my moonstone, I thought.

I skipped the dishes and worked on my tapestry. Of all crazy things, I saw a live spider sitting boldly in the middle of my canvas. Without thinking, I did what I always did. I shook the spider onto the floor as hard as I could and then stepped on it. I did it as automatically as I slap a mosquito when it's biting me.

Seconds later I realized I had blundered again, only it was worse this time, because I thought I had learned about spiders. Wasn't that what the night of the star goddess was all about? By becoming a spider, I went into the center of my fear. That should have released me, shouldn't it?

Ask me, I'll tell you. Spiders are great and wonderful creatures. I know I don't need to be afraid of them. My consciousness is raised. But where was the action to demonstrate the change in me? I sat down before my canvas and promised myself and spiders everywhere that I would never kill another spider. I must put an end to this vicious, mindless behavior, I thought. I must.

To confirm this promise, I hooked a spider with brown yarn into the center of my canvas. I put it on the wing of what looked like a yellow space ship. I hoped that each time I saw the spider, it would remind me not to be afraid, not just of spiders, but of any living thing, that it would remind me to let go of old fears, to listen respectfully, and to try to open my heart.

Next, I had to find another live spider so I could practice my new resolution. I wished I could be more like Doc. He actually strokes his water spiders on the head as he watches the sun go down,

Aron said I would have as many opportunities to learn from a spider as I needed. I wondered if he knew my parents would be coming back soon. They would think Aron was exceptionally strange if he made himself known to them.

I looked everywhere for a live spider. I looked in my slippers. I checked my washcloth (spiders get thirsty, too). I even looked in the cereal boxes. All I found was one dead spider in the outhouse.

Before long, I tired of my search and put all thoughts of spiders aside -- for the time being. The day was too beautiful to go on conducting a spider hunt, despite my resolution of intent. It was a typical Canadian late summer day: warm sun, light wind, blue sky, cool water. I wanted to be alone with my thoughts.

I put on a pink and white checked one piece bathing suit and a big straw hat, grabbed a lawn chair, and went out onto one of the front rocks at the edge of the point. I had a craving to lie back and enjoy the day -- at least for a little while before I began my chores. There was nothing I liked more than letting the sun open my pores and then diving into the ice cold lake, feeling the water close them.

I lay in the sun until I tingled with vitamin D. Then I tossed my big sun hat onto the lawn chair, walked to the edge of the rock, and dove into the lake. The first dive was always the best one.

I didn't like to touch bottom after a dive, so I automatically struck out into the lake toward Gull Rock, a mound of ancient granite left by the glaciers many eons ago. I was only mildly concerned I was disobeying my parents' orders: "Do not swim out to Gull Rock alone -- it's too far -- you might get a cramp -- something might happen." I paid their warnings no heed; after all, everyone knew I was a very good swimmer.

Gull Rock rises out of the lake like a baby iceberg, about 50 yards from shore. Above the surface, it is about as big around as my father's rubber boat. I named it Gull Rock because there were usually gulls sitting on it.

The wind was kicking up, but it wasn't strong enough to worry me or make me change my mind. I badly wanted a cooling swim, so I swam on. My parents didn't need to know.

Cassie watched from shore. She is not a swimming dog.

The water is my second home. I discovered a long time ago that with less effort I could go farther with each stroke. I don't get nearly as winded or tired as I do when I hurry. By swimming "with" the water, I can swim forever. I have been told I swim more like a cruise ship than a speed boat.

I swam slowly and steadily and let the water support me the way I know to do. I tried to think about all the lessons of the frog as I swam: don't tighten, let go, trust all that is.

Eventually I reached good old dependable Gull Rock, safe and sound. However, there were no gulls to greet me, which was highly unusual -- a sign of changing weather I should have noted.

I hung on to the rock and rested. As I pressed my body into one of the rock's contours, I was surprised to realize the rock was alive, too. Oh my, I thought, I have found yet another teacher!

"Hi, Gull Rock," I said. "How are you today? Do you have a message for me?"

The rock said nothing in reply. It is always very friendly, but I can't recall that it has ever spoken in a language I can understand. I feel certain if it were ever to speak, it would do so with grunts or monosyllabic sounds. It is too wise, too old, and too knowing to answer with words. It has been there a long time.

When I moved out of my reverie with the rock, I realized the wind was stronger than when I set out. Again, I wasn't worried. I'd been swimming on much windier days than this one.

Since it was such a beautiful day, I decided that instead of swimming straight back to shore, I'd swim over to the three little islands that Doc called the Three Sisters, 50 yards or so away from Gull Rock but no farther from shore.

The wind felt like a rain wind. I couldn't understand why. There wasn't a cloud in the sky.

I said goodbye to Gull Rock and pushed off, heading toward the Three Sisters. I had to swim against the wind in that direction, which wasn't as much fun but did give me a better workout. Some of the waves rushed over my face when I was breathing in new air, forcing water into my mouth and down into my chest. When I spat the water out, I felt like a small white whale.

A speed boat whammed and bammed its way past. Wham and bam! That's the sound motor boats make when the waves are high. Big power boats don't belong on this lake. Any jerk knows that. Wham bam, wham bam! The sound faded away as I continued to swim.

Whoosh! A huge wave splashed over my head. The wave came from the wake of that blasted, oversized motor boat. I choked, I coughed and I sputtered. I couldn't catch my breath. I couldn't take in air through my mouth or my nose. I felt as if my wind pipe had closed.

I began to thrash around, trying to catch my breath, reverting to the doggie paddle I taught myself when I was really little.

I panicked. Gull Rock looked far away. The Three Sisters looked farther away. Land looked even farther away. I decided the smart thing to do was to head directly back to shore. But how could I go anywhere if I couldn't get any air into my lungs?

What was I to do? Doc couldn't see me from his cottage. Most of the people with cottages on the lake were weekend people, and this was a Wednesday. The dratted speed boat was far away. I was alone.

Those thoughts crowded my brain. I didn't review my life the way people in the movies do when they are scared, but I began to wonder if I might not make it back to shore.

I tried floating on my back on top of the water. Floating is the easiest thing I know to do when I can't catch my breath. But now the wind was stronger. Wave after wave washed over me. My feelings of panic increased.

Suddenly, there were big black clouds in the sky, and the sun disappeared behind them. I found if I breathed through my nose, a little air burst through. I breathed slowly and deeply, in and out, in and out. I had no energy to scream for help; even if I had, no one would have heard me over the howling wind.

Don't tighten! Let go! Trust all that is!

Where was all that is now? I didn't know who or what to trust. I realized I might drown. My tired body felt heavy with fear. Come on all that is, start working! Aron, you're not going to let me die, are you?

Don't give up! I told myself. I am a good swimmer. I know these waters well. Ordinarily I could swim the distance to shore with one arm. Stop tightening. The water will hold me up.

I stayed on my back and struggled to do the back stroke. More waves washed over my face. My arms moved faster than they needed to, and I kicked my legs wildly. I got more and more desperate for air.

I thought about the fly. I thought about the frogs. I thought about the turtles. I thought about the star goddess. Where were all my teachers now? Everything I learned during the preceding week seemed to be gone.

I rolled over on my front side to see shore. It looked a whole football field away.

Take it easy, don't tighten, let go and trust. Trust what?

I tried swimming the breast stroke for a while. That meant I could keep my head out of the water a little longer. It was still hard to breathe.

I thought of the turtles again. They would never put themselves in such a predicament.

I kicked the frog kick hard until my knees ached. I barely inhaled enough oxygen to keep going.

I felt myself growing weaker. My fear grew. Fear changed my relationship with everything.

The wind is too strong, I thought. I was making very little progress. I no longer trusted the lake, the water, the wind. I couldn't trust all that is.

And I didn't trust myself. Why hadn't I heeded my parents' warning not to swim to Gull Rock alone?

Maybe that was why I wasn't able to see the star goddess the night before. I wasn't worthy.

If only Doc could see me and come to rescue me.

The waves seemed over two feet high. They kept washing over my head. Whitecaps were everywhere. My chest ached as I fought to push fresh oxygen into my lungs. Fear kept me low in the water.

I was in despair.

Then, incredibly, I saw a loon in the water five feet ahead of me toward shore. A tiny voice inside me said, "Listen! Move inward and listen!"

I made myself try.

Slowly, ever so slowly, I took a good, full breath of air, and then another. I moved into an inner space. My world slowed down; I felt the grip of fear loosen. I kept my concentration inside me because I knew that was where I needed to be.

Then I understood. My teacher had come.

A loon looks like a duck. It is a superb swimmer, and can swim below the water with as much ease as above, which most ducks can't do.

Whenever danger is near -- when a boat or a person comes too close -- a loon disappears under the surface of the lake, to resurface sometimes yards and yards away.

I swam toward the loon. Five feet? I could swim five feet. My lungs received enough air to do that.

When I almost reached the loon, it disappeared under the water.

But in a stroke's time, the loon reappeared. Once more it was just five feet ahead of me. That was five feet closer to shore.

Once more I swam toward the loon.

Don't tighten. Let go. Trust all that is! Now I was finally beginning to understand those words.

The loon disappeared under the water, then reappeared again another five feet closer to shore.

Again, it stayed ahead of me until I almost caught up with it, and then it dove down under the water.

All that is! It's in the loon, I thought.

Then I knew: all that is is in me!

My swimming became more trusting. I was not nearly as afraid as I had been. I kept my eyes on the head of the loon with its red, beady eyes. The white lines around its neck made the loon look like a priest.

Trust.

I trusted all that is in the loon. That meant I was trusting all that is in me. I suddenly felt I could do anything. I knew in my heart I could make it to shore. I knew I was going to be all right.

The loon and I swam together that way, ever closer to shore, until I put my feet down and touched the rocky bottom. After a flap of its wings, the loon slipped away under the water.

The rocky bottom and the lake grass around my legs felt heaven-sent. Tears gushed from my eyes. I coughed water and phlegm out of my lungs. I stood up to say thank you to the loon. I did it! We did it!

Thank you, all that is,
in the loon,
in the lake,
in Aron,
in me.

Cassie greeted me ecstatically.

Out on the lake, the loon bobbed up and down like a cork on the crest of each wave. I could tell it trusted all that is as it stretched its neck long.

"Caw, keeee…caw," the loon called.

I climbed up on the rock I had started from -- hours ago, or so it seemed.

"Caw…keeee… swe…se…se!"

At last I could feel what Aron meant when he said my teachers were ever present. I was so grateful I said thank you, thank you to everything that moved or breathed around me.

Thank you, big pine trees.

Thank you, Cassie.

Thank you, chipmunk running over the rocks.

I sat down in the lawn chair to stop shaking. I gave more thanks. The wind was blowing hard, too hard for even the hardiest of swimmers. I had never seen the lake so agitated.

I wrapped the towel around me to get warm. My chattering teeth made me sound like a nervous woodpecker.

The sun was still behind big black clouds. The rock under me held some residual heat, but the air was cool.

A drop of something wet splashed on my nose. I wiped it off, looking at my hand suspiciously, wondering if it fell from a bird. Then a drop landed on my forehead, and another on my left knee. It was raining. The black clouds had been holding rain.

Out on the lake, the loon immediately announced the rain to all listening creatures with an excited call.

I gathered my sun hat and my towel, left the chair on the rock, called Cassie to come with me, and hurried inside the cottage. As soon as I closed the door, it began to pour -- not just a light little rain, but a serious downpour.

I tightened the towel around my shoulders and went over to the sink. I reached for a mug as I brewed tea. I was terribly chilled, and felt a bit disoriented after my ordeal in the lake.

At the sink, my mind was still on rain clouds and big waves. I absently took the mug in hand. Then I felt it. A spider crept out of the mug and dashed on to my wrist. And there it stayed. It was brown, like Charlotte.

"Ugh!"

To think I might have swallowed it. Again, ugh!

I put the mug down with a crash and reflexively brushed the spider onto the floor. I raised my foot to stamp on it, but suddenly stopped. My foot stayed suspended in the air.

Oh, no! I'd almost done it again. Useless, thankless me. After all I had been given. All spiders everywhere must know I'd almost broken my promise to them. Who would want to teach me now?

I immediately went down on my hands and knees to look for the bruised spider. It was no longer in sight. I hoped and prayed I would not step on it.

Would I never change, I asked myself as I crawled around? The room was so dark from the rain clouds that I reached to the log table for a flashlight.

"Charlotte! Here, Charlotte! I'm sorry, so very, very sorry."

When a spider is frightened or hurt, it curls up into a ball and makes itself very small. When it thinks it is safe, it creeps away. I learned that when I was a spider.

I moved the beam of the flashlight around, into the cracks on the floor. I put on my glasses so I could see better. Please don't be dead, sweet Charlotte. Please!

Way over beneath the broiler drawer under the oven, I saw a spider. I was sure it was the very same spider. It was so small it looked like a crumb from a piece of toast. "Please be all right," I pleaded.

As gently as I could, I picked up the curled-up spider with a tissue. I prayed for its good health.

"Okay, spider. I'm trying not to be afraid of you. Truly, I'm doing my best. I hope it's good enough."

My body stiffened in spite of my good intentions.

"I'm going to put you out under the stairs of the porch where you won't feel the rain. In the future, please try making your home under the cottage instead of in it with me."

I hoped when I put it down I'd be able to see it wiggle or maybe crawl into hiding, so I'd know it was alive.

I opened the back door, and quickly stepped out. I moved fast, fearful the spider might slip out of the tissue and start crawling back over my wrist. The rain poured down my back.

I paused a moment. In my hand, in the tissue, was one of my teachers, another life-form, a creature who was trying to be happy as I was. The spider was as fearful at that moment as I had been out on the lake.

"Trust all that is, friend Charlotte!"

I gently shook the tissue under the bottom step, and the spider dropped to the ground.

"Go on, Charlotte! Be free!"

The spider didn't move. I sang to the spider.

THERE'S A LIGHT AROUND YOU

GUIDING YOU TO SEE.

It was the song Aron sang in my bedroom earlier in the week.

NOW THE LIGHT'S WITHIN YOU.
The spider twitched. It was alive.

TEACHING YOU TO BE.

Pick up the spider, I said to myself. It is too wet under the stairs; pick up the spider and put it farther under the cottage.

I couldn't.

I began to cry.

A tear splashed down near the spider, then another, and another, much warmer and saltier than rain drops.

I stood up to go back into the cottage. My inner voice spoke again: "Pick up the spider and put it where you know it will be safe and dry."

I bent back down. The spider was still rolled tightly in its little ball, looking as if it had no legs.

I couldn't touch it.

I couldn't.

I couldn't.

I wouldn't.

"Remember how it felt," my inner voice continued, "being a spider, dancing as a spider, climbing as a spider, swinging from the birch tree as a spider. Remember how full and special you felt?"

It was useless.

"I'll never truly learn anything. I'll never change," I said out loud.

"You became a spider and you came back changed," my inner voice said. "You became one with the lake, one with the loon, one with all that is, and again you were changed. Now prove it to yourself. Do it!"

I moved inward, as I did in the lake. I saw the spider's pain. Its whole body was cringing and tightening, the way my mouth does when I suck a lemon.

I couldn't touch it.

I stood up, went into the cottage and slammed the door.

I had failed. I had been shown so much; I had learned so much; but again I had failed.

At least I didn't kill it, I thought. I must be getting a little better. But that gave me no consolation. I felt utterly dejected. I felt as terrible as I did when Lewis, my parakeet, died at the beginning of the summer.

The rain continued. The sun shone on the other side of the lake.

"It makes no difference! I'm just a dumb, stupid, insensitive person. Who cares about spiders, anyway? Who cares if it rains or not? Who wants to sit in the sun anymore? I don't."

I was too ornery to do anything but moan and feel sorry for myself. I didn't deserve the comfort the sun could bring. I went to the table and sat down to mope.

No wonder I had to give my moonstone back. I was not worthy of it. I wished my parents would come and take me away from this dreadful place.

I put my head down on my arm. I couldn't even cry. I picked up the pencil by my shopping list, and began to draw little pictures beside the items on the list.

Apples

Bananas.

Stamps.

Then I drew some little loops:

I'd drawn loops like those since I was little. Loops that went on forever. I let the loops circle up near the apple at the top of my list.

Suddenly, my pencil took on an energy that was unfamiliar. It wanted to go one way while I wanted to go another.

"Come on," I said to the pencil. "Are you against me, too?"

The pencil insisted, or the energy moving through the pencil insisted. I kept holding it and watching it as it slowly formed two words: "Dear One."

Automatic writing! The pencil paused. I ripped my shopping list and the loops from the pad and turned to a clean sheet. I had an overwhelming urge to write myself a letter. The pencil started again.

"Dear One, cheer up! Keep listening! You are doing fine, a step at a time. You learn at your own rate."

Suddenly, I began to understand.

I wanted to change everything at once. That was an impossible expectation. Change is an ongoing process. The fly and the petals of the water lily should have taught me that. Opening my heart to spiders must be an ongoing process, too.

The writing continued. "Your feelings are catching up with your thoughts. Be patient. Try to notice all the many little changes you do make along the way."

It was hard to see little changes when all I wanted were big ones.

More automatic writing: "The spider is teaching you about honoring all life. To honor all life, you must honor yourself first."

That was the key. Other people couldn't like me the way I was if I didn't like myself. And I couldn't like myself if I went on killing spiders.

More automatic writing: "Praise each tear you gave to the spider. Praise yourself for caring more and behaving differently."

"Will I then learn the words to the turtle song?" I wanted to know.

There was no answer to that question, only "Your loving U.P. Aron."

"Wow! I get it!" I shouted. "Aron has been in me all this time. So have the eagle, the turtles, the loon, maybe even the star goddess."

More automatic writing: "P.S. When you put down this pencil, turn your tapestry around and around and look at it from a different perspective."

The pencil stopped moving. I put it down and looked at the four or five sheets of paper before me. The handwriting was much bigger and bolder than my usual writing. Many of the words looked as if they were written by a small child.

Aron was right. Rather, I was right, we were right. I was changing. I didn't kill the spider. I did pick it up and take it outside. Something was clearly shifting.

I heard my own praise. I was beginning to feel better, a lot better.

I glanced at my tapestry and all its little pieces of yarn hooked into the canvas. I turned my tapestry around and looked at it upside-down.

I couldn't believe what I saw.

What I thought was a white bird was no longer a white bird. It was hair, the hair on the head of a very old and wise person wearing three feathers. The person was emerging out of the bottom of the canvas. It was Aron, I was sure, smoking his peace pipe. What I thought was a yellow space ship was a light radiating from the top of Aron's head. The lines and squares were a great big spider web.

At the top right corner was the beginning of a rainbow. A few days ago, when looking at the tapestry the other way up, I thought it was a road.

The things I thought were little triangles or trees were now decorations on a tepee, and the little white clouds were puffs of smoke from Aron's pipe.

I realized the tapestry was finished.

The rainbow in the tapestry held my attention. I began to feel a slight buzz -- a signal that said to be alert. I was getting better at staying alert and listening to what I felt.

I looked outside. I smelled sage. The sun shone down on my side of the lake. I saw colors in the sky that I rarely saw. For once I gave myself no time to impose old thoughts on new. I ran out the door.

There was still a slight breeze that felt so good. Now the sun seemed fully out, but it continued to rain.

The smell of sage got stronger. The pine trees seemed to lean away from each other, making the path wider so I could get to the edge of the lake faster.

Cassie watched from beneath her favorite tree, and even the cats appeared from under the cottage to stare.

"There has to be a rainbow," I murmured to myself. "There has to be!"

The lake, now calm, shimmered with excitement. I stood at the far edge of the largest rock, without sunglasses and without my sun hat. I stood boldly in the light.

Everything looked blurry because of the big drops of rain that were falling into my eyes. I scanned the opposite shore for a piece of a rainbow.

I repeated, "There must be one! There has to be one!"

Nothing. All I saw was the part-blue part-gray sky. The rain kept falling and the sun kept shining.

I lay down on the rock and looked up behind the cottage, back toward the woods. I didn't see a rainbow, but I liked the way the rock felt on my back and shoulders, all wet and warm.

I stayed there quietly, with my arms open wide, as my eyes alternately opened and closed. My arms felt like eagle wings, as if I, too, were preparing for flight. I was smiling, but I wasn't sure why. Maybe it was because I was happy, feeling good about myself in a fully wakeful state. The sun was glaringly white. A new thought flashed into my mind: could I be lying in the eye in the moonstone?

In the haze and the glare, I began to see a rainbow forming. Then I saw another.

They both began at the north end of the lake, one a big archway and another smaller one nestled inside it.

But there was more. It looked as if the ends of the double rainbows were coming down onto the rock where I was lying!

The buzz increased.

Everyone knows there is a pot of gold at the end of a rainbow. Did that mean there was a pot of gold where I lay, maybe two?

Could I be the pot of gold?

The buzz was out of control.

The rainbows stretched long to reach me. The sun warmed my chest. I felt a sprinkling of multi-colored light around me. For the first time in my life, I felt chosen for something.

I lay on the rock, as open to the sun as I could be. I wanted to absorb and bathe myself in all the colors of the rainbows above me.

The water from the lake lapped gently against the rock, periodically touching the tips of my fingers as I stretched long and wide. I couldn't have been more open. The water blessed me with its cool energy. The rock held me as an honored friend.

My heart got warmer and warmer. I arched my back high and lifted my chest to the sun.

Suddenly, I shouted: "I am the pot of gold!"

A light from my heart pushed to be released out of every opening of my body -- my eyes, my ears, my nose, my skin.

I laughed out loud as I repeated "I'm the pot of gold!" over and over again.

"I'm the pot of gold. I'm the pot of gold. I'm the pot of gold!

"No! I'm the pot. All that is is the gold.

"I'm the pot filled with gold!

"I'm worthy.

"I'm the pot holding all that is!"

My chest lifted higher and higher. Laughter bubbled out of me in ripples. Great belly laughs came next.

A spider walked onto my hand, up my arm, and settled on my chest. Immediately I moved inside myself.

I saw the spider.

I acknowledged it.

We acknowledged each other.

The spider winked. I sent it love. I still didn't want to touch it. But that was all right. I honored it with tender thoughts and praised myself for that. The spider walked on.

By seeing all that is in me, I could see it in everything around me, even the spider.

As my back arched, my arms stretched yet wider to the side.

"I am.

"I am one with all that is.

"I am one with all that is and all life."

I laughed with pure joy. My eyes burned from the light inside me meeting the light outside.

My chest lifted high, my heart cavity widened. Then slowly, I felt an opening down the center of my breast bone. My ribs separated, and I called: "Eya!" I was unfolding like the water lily. I was the last two petals of the star goddess opening. Instantly, I began to sing:

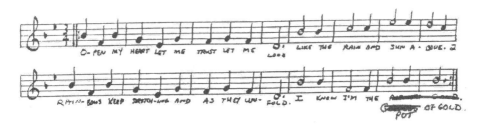

I sang it again and again, louder each time.

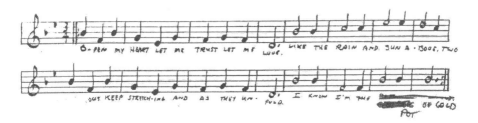

The third time I sang it, I realized I was singing the turtle song. I knew the words! I was finally open enough to receive them.

Open my heart, let me trust, let me love,
Like the rain and sun above.
Two rainbows reach toward me and as they unfold,
I know I'm the pot of gold.

No, that was wrong. I am the pot. All that is is the gold. I would have to change the words in that part of the song. Tomorrow.

I sang higher now, reaching notes I thought I would never sing. I sang to an eagle hovering above me. It circled low over my head, flying with the verve and style of Aron. I knew the eagle was Aron, and that it and he were inside of me. I said a prayer to all things that fly.

Then I sang to the sun, the moon, the clouds.

I sang to the frogs. I sang to the turtles. My heart was hot. My body was shifting and changing. I could see all of me. None of my secrets scared me anymore. The light inside me moved and danced.

I sang to the fish. I sang to Cassie, Lizzie and Twyla, sitting like a choir under the big pine tree. I sang to the deer mouse, looking out from the woodpile.

"Will I ever be this happy again?"

I called to Aron the eagle, and listened for the knowing I knew would be coming my way.

A voice inside me said, "If you shake off fear about people not liking you, and you decide you no longer need to be punished by the God of thunderstorms, and you are clear you are not the ghost maiden and you are not even like her -- then I declare you to be worthy of the favor of the star goddess."

I sighed a deep sigh.

Aron the eagle went on. "Know you are blessed, guided, unconditionally loved, safe, and divinely taught in the dream or trance state."

I tried hard to memorize those words.

"Know these things," Aron the eagle said as he glided back and forth above me. "Know the answers you seek are in you, and reach out and be love, be trust, and be peace."

I gave my weight to the rock. I dipped my fingertips into the lake and splashed water onto my forehead. I blessed myself, all of myself, with this sacred water.

"Kya! Kya!"

The eagle went flying by. I thought of the moonstone. I wondered if the star goddess had claimed it last night; I hoped she had. If not, perhaps the eagle had it and would deliver it to the next needy person.

The eagle disappeared from sight. I had a feeling I would not see Aron the eagle again.

I put my hand on the pouch on my chest where the moonstone used to be. My heart quivered with new life.

In that moment, I knew my heart was open.

In that moment, I was happy, and I was free. I knew my lesson was to maintain those feelings of wellness and goodness. I knew it wouldn't be easy, but I was on my way. I couldn't ask for anything more. To celebrate, I fell asleep.

CHAPTER SEVEN

Three hours after my nap on the rock, my parents returned. By then I had managed to get the dishes done.

The cottage looked as good as it did when my mother was in charge.

They reported Granny Rose was feeling better. They said they had missed me a lot. I knew they had. I missed them, too, more than I thought I would. During my time alone, I discovered just how much I loved them.

"What did you do while you had the cottage to yourself?" they asked. "Mrs. McCrae said something about your throwing her frogs away. What was that about?"

I didn't know what to say, so I sat and grinned like the proverbial Cheshire cat.

"When you're ready to talk," said my father, "I'm ready to listen. Meanwhile, I'll ask Doc to fill us in."

At which point he stood up and started to collect his casting gear so he could catch several small mouth bass for dinner.

My mother was going nowhere. She was glad to be back at the cottage and reconnected with me. She heated some water for tea. She kept looking at me, as only a mother can, out of the corner of her eye, as if she were trying to jump into my head so I'd tell her about my adventures. Needless to say, I wouldn't let her go there. Doc would understand, but no one else would.

"We have a present for you," my father said before he stepped out of the cottage.

"A present?" I asked.

"Yes," my mother answered. "Just a little something."

"And I have a present for you, too," I said. "Look and see. My tapestry almost hooked itself. And, I'm happy to say, I finished it today. Isn't it pretty?"

Of course, Mom and Dad ohhed and ahhed, although I must say they really seemed to like it. My mother was particularly pleased I had finished something I started.

My father put his hand in his side pocket and pulled out a small envelope.

"Close both your eyes," he insisted. He looked as if he were holding something precious.

"And what you get will be a surprise," added my mom playfully.

So I closed my eyes. I had a familiar feeling. What was it?

My father placed something in my right palm. It was warm. I recognized the feeling immediately. I opened my eyes. It was a moonstone. Not just any old moonstone, but my moonstone!

The moonstone was the only precious gem I had ever heard of that felt warm to the touch.

My moonstone was the only moonstone I knew of that had an eye etched at the top end of the stone.

I gasped. I couldn't believe what I was seeing. I felt myself growing taller and stronger. I felt as though a whole new me were being created. I loved the feeling. I wanted it to last forever. It should, I thought, if I'm careful not to misplace this mysterious, magical moonstone again.

"Where did you get it?" I asked. "How could you possibly know this is the best present in the world?!"

"Ah," my father said, "it made me think of you and Doc and the kind of thing that gives you both such pleasure. He collects stones. You collect stones. I felt confident this little beauty might be just the right thing for you."

I pulled my small pouch out from under my sweatshirt.

"Thank you so much!" I said.

"You're welcome," my parents said in chorus as they watched me place the moonstone in the small pouch.

"This is the best present ever," I kept repeating. "Where in the world did you find it?"

My father answered that question, too. "I got it from a man on a Toronto street corner who looked like a lumberjack. He had on a black and red checked wool jacket. He said he found this particular stone on a sandy flat next to the water's edge, where turtles drop their eggs. I'm glad you like it. The lumberjack would be pleased, too. He wouldn't let me pay him, you know."

I began to feel a little faint.

"Are you okay, dear?" my mother asked. "Would you like some tea?"

I shook my head no. I was in a state of shock.

The moonstone had just given me the perfect ending of a perfect day.

I went into my bedroom. I had no urge to ask another question. Can you believe it? I, the queen of questions?

EPILOGUE

After my time alone in our cottage on a lake in the Canadian woods, my life has never been the same. My parents noticed something was different about me right away. They said I had done a lot of growing up. Just the kind of thing parents would say, aye? They were partially right, but not completely right. My whole world had expanded.

Doc knew. He knew everything before I had a chance to tell him any of the details. He knew about my visitors. He knew about the turtles. He knew about Aron. He knew about the eagle. He knew about the star goddess. He knew about the moonstone. He knew everything! Doc said, "Welcome to my world, Rosalie Ann."

Oh my, the way he said my name brought tears to my eyes. He didn't say my full name in anger the way my parents did when I did something wrong. Instead, he inferred I had finally grown into my given name. Then he gave me a smile, the likes of which I had never before received from him. I will always think of Doc and Aron as my spiritual advisors.

Shortly after my parents returned from their time away, I overheard my father talking to Doc down on our dock while they were casting for small mouth bass. My father said to Doc, "Do you think we did the right thing, letting Rosie stay in the cottage alone?"

"Oh yes," answered Doc. "You knew I'd keep an eye on her, although I must say she never needed me, not really. You should be proud of her. She has a good head on her shoulders. Not to worry."

That was all he said.

"Thanks for looking after my little girl," said my father. I could feel Doc's smile. It was a smile that said to my father, "No matter how much learning your daughter does, she will always be your little girl."

Of course, I wanted to hear more. But the two men went on to another subject. Fish.

I never did tell my mother and father much about what happened to me while they were away in Toronto. There was so much they wouldn't have understood. They would have scolded me for letting the stranger in the house on that stormy night, my being alone and all.

Aron is always with me -- in the city or out of the city, at the lake or not at the lake. Aron's my best friend.

One time my mother heard me talking to him. I was in my room with the door closed and thought I was alone. When she questioned me about who I was talking to,

I felt I had no choice but to tell her about him -- not everything, but something.

When I finished, my mother looked at me seriously and said, "Many children have imaginary playmates (I could feel my eyes rolling up to the ceiling -- was she going to lecture me?), which is all well and good. Just promise me you won't talk about Aron in school. I don't think your teachers would understand."

I promised.

*

Now that I am older, I know there are many things I may never fully understand. The mystery of the moonstone is one of them. However, I always wear my moonstone in my pouch, next to my heart.

THE END

20215894R00099

Made in the USA
Middletown, DE
19 May 2015